Published in 2021 by Exhale Publishing
Copyright © Careen Latoya Lawrence

Exhale Publishing is part of 4D-House Ltd.

Prepared for publishing by Careen Latoya Lawrence
Editor: Olivia Newnham
Illustrator: Camilla Daniel

A CIP catalogue record for this title is available from the British Library.

ISBN: 978-1-5272-9904-7

LOVE IN BLACK
Careen Latoya Lawrence

Exhale Publishing

LOVE IN BLACK

Careen Latoya Lawrence

Acknowledgements

First and foremost, my thanks goes to God. My ability to write and even publish this book under my company, that's from Him. This book has been through a lot since being started in 2019 and now, by the grace of God, it's here.

Secondly, I would like to say thanks to all the Black couples out there. I don't always see many of you in public, but I guess that's because you aren't out in the the world displaying your relationship. That being said, my model Black couples, my parents and my cousin Kimika and her husband Wale, helped me when thinking about what Black couples look like. I chose to write this book because I noticed I was seeing a lot more white couples, or interracial couples in public, but not many Blacks. I wanted to then explore not only the romantic relationship, but that bit more, the self-love, the familial love. I would like to thank my model couples mentioned as they have a level of self-love which I'm sure helps them with navigating through their love life and their marriages.

I would also like to thank everyone who has supported me on this journey. In particular, there are six Queens I feel deserve to be mentioned, one from the UK, who, thanks to Covid, became a great support system for me throughout this process. The first Queen I'd like to thank is Simonne (UK) whom I met just before the pandemic. When I was on a writing spree during lockdown, I would give her an update as to how many words I had written. Honestly, how Simonne put up with my constant updates, I have no clue. But there were days I found it difficult to continue and she encouraged me to keep pushing.

I would like to thank my Writers Block sisters, Felicia Cade (USA), Ciani Marie (USA), and Cephorah (South Africa). These ladies said yes to me when I was going through a dry spell with my writing and we formed a group who met three times a week while the pandemic was causing havoc. Our time together was spent talking, writing, and giving each other feedback.

Next, Azia Monae (USA), had at one point become my soundboard. She would listen to sections at a time and give her feedback, it would be wrong of me not to say thanks. Azia's favourite in this book is definitely the section which compares friends to trees. The sixth and final Queen is Claire 'Lethal Poet' Vilain (USA). Claire has been a fabulous support system for me. This Queen has encouraged and motivated me, always cheering for me. Had it not been for Covid and the world being forced to go into lockdown mode, I would never have known about any of these ladies, besides Simonne and Felicia. I can't even think about what it would have been like for me had Covid not happened.

My final thank you goes to Olivia Newnham, my friend and editor. She has been my editor since my second book and I can't tell you how amazing she is! The suggestions she has made within editing have been phenomenal and it's as though she knows my mind. I know I would not have been able to do this without her. The hours she devoted to editing this book, to my mind, makes her a superhero. Olivia, you rock! It's been a tough journey, but you helped me despite the world around. Thank you.

Don't think I've forgotten about you, the reader, my critic. You who have either bought this book, or have been gifted a copy and have sat down to delve into it, I would like to thank you for your time. This is different, if you're a returning reader, you will see the difference, I've not just written poetry, I've written my first novel. You mean a lot to me. Getting this far, knowing that you will continue. Thank you. For those who will spread the word and encourage friends and family to get a copy, thank you.

Trigger Warning

Before you go any further, I'd love for you to read this. I guess we can say this is a trigger warning for reasons that will be below.

Over the past number of years, going to open mics and with the pandemic, doing virtual open mics, one thing stands out which is dissimilar from the days when I had just started performing; a valuable lesson on my part, and that is giving trigger warnings.

I have friends who have endured some unfortunate circumstances, and in their honour, it wouldn't be right if I didn't do this.

This book contains themes such as incest, sexual abuse, self-harm and miscarriage. These themes are referenced implicitly and explicitly throughout the book, and this is just a heads up that you may tread carefully as you read.

Niyah's story isn't one I expect to be easily digested. She has a past, one of which narrates her current state of being. It is what's helped her to become better in aspects of her life. I want you, the reader, to be aware that there may be some skimming over paragraphs.

Lastly, this is not a book for under 16s. There are some things I do not want to expose them to. There is a small voice in me screaming to say, under 18s, keep the book away from under 18s. Parental discretion is advised. If you believe your child can read this under 18 or 16, it's your ruling against mine, but I must add words of warning.

Love in Black is far from 'Free' and 'Naked Lenses'. This book is a woman's journey; some of the story talks about her sexual experience in a bit of depth. It is an every woman kind of book. There are pieces of a world of women within it.

I hope I haven't deterred you, and I hope you do enjoy reading as much as I've enjoyed writing.

Jul. 2019

Jul.2019

Thursday 25th July 2019

Dear Orion,

When it all comes down to the final stages of wondering, we realise that love is an intricate detail, difficult to be unpicked or researched for understanding. We can look within ourselves and question why we either love so easily or why we find it difficult to do so; however, we have yet to grasp what love really means and how we can measure it effectively.

Can love be measured by kisses planted on cheeks, or how long we can spend together in silence? Better yet, is love a synonym for trust, to be able to unrequitedly offer your time, moments, emotions and thoughts while expecting that your commitment is handled with care?

How I may define this adorned and great gift will be different from your views and opinions. Where I say it starts may not match up with your beliefs, but we all know it begins somewhere, and it also has to end. Then there is hate.

Hatred is the foundation on which many families have been built. Many black families, to be precise. Having lost the true essence of love to slavery, we have unknowingly joined forces with this poisonous matter that has transformed our DNA; Distinctive Neural Assembly. How we perceive each other is no longer the pure form before the mistreatment of our ancestors, inhumane.

Families are trying to find ways to mend, and others have given up on everyone but themselves. Essentially, it results from not knowing the truth, trying to base our lives on what was written from the imagination. You could argue that one's imagination correlates with the spiritual world. However, those who are creators were blessed with this gift of subconsciously knowing what has come before.

If this is the case, why are few black families shown to be living harmoniously with each other on TV? The idea that black families can be well off and not act as barbaric now has light shining on it. Yay to there now being representations of successful black families, but this still is not enough. Is it not about time that someone decides to show the world that we can make it out of the ghettos into which we were thrown? Is it not about time that someone chooses to create a world on screens to show that the individual who made it out has come back to help free those who are still within?

If we start to see these things, then situations will change. No longer will Lewisham be the most dangerous area. No longer will black children constantly be excluded from schools. No longer will black men need to feel that they have to date outside of our race to protect their egos that they may not feel threatened. No longer will black women feel they need to date a white man to be secure and happy.

When you grow up in Lewisham, you do not recognise that self-love is lost unless your parents have instilled it in you. Can we even say self-love is something that can be instilled? Is it an intrinsic or a learnt behaviour? Whatever the case, I've seen enough men loitering, teaching boys how to 'shot', how to shift drugs without being caught. Too many of the boys I knew turned out to be drug dealers, and few treated women well.

Black women were always at a loss. With that climate, there was no respect given to them. Amongst themselves, they spoke about being happy by getting in a relationship with a white man. They wholeheartedly believed that white was the light. Black men had it more challenging. The good ones, those who knew how to treat women, were shut down on more occasions than they could count, so they too looked into dating outside the race. Hard to be mad at them for their choices. We know this goes way back with all that is happening, thus leaving us with questions about happiness.

What is happiness? Is happiness the definition of love? Can happiness only be found in relationships? Who is it that teaches us to be happy?

We need more to go on to find the answers.

The world needs many more present historical figures, those willing to stand amid this fog-filled world. I need more black figures to be the root from which self-loving families can grow. I know I may not see it in my life, but my children and grandchildren may see it. I would love to have folks who can stand with me; stand firm, and work for what we once had.

Some may not realise it, but I believe that love in its purest form allows us to be at peace without anxieties of being misinformed by those we say we love, mistreated, and cheated on by our partners in relationships. At what point does it become pure love? I can't precisely say, but I'm sure it still exists.

I feel I am delusional, having had a difficult time finding someone I can say I love. Life has dealt me so many hands I have lost, yet I am still hopeful that I will find someone or they find me in due time.

Growing up, I always wondered what it was that caused the breakdown in relationships. Though I saw and knew of other children from two-parent homes, I feel as though I knew of a similar number from single-parent backgrounds. As I've gotten older, I've seen enough propaganda showing that blacks cannot maintain healthy relationships because it is the expected stereotype.

We are afraid to remain together and try when we know the world is ready to criticise us. To be told in school that you cannot and will not achieve, to be jeered by friends when we like someone, to be presented with broken homes on TV; can anyone blame us for our fear?

I am at an age I believe the need for me to unearth misconceptions is imperative. I need to be able to come to terms with what goes wrong before I can move forward. I have traits I would not want to pass on to my children, nor would I want to project them onto my future partner.

My name is Niyah Adenike Thomas, and I have always been told that I am special. My grandmother has always sat me at her feet to tell me stories of her childhood and my mother's childhood. Papa, my grandfather, has always sat me on his lap and, without fail, explained to me what it is that my name means. My grandmother's childhood, married with the meaning of my first and middle name, has made Papa believe that I am the one who will bring change to our family.

What Papa failed to tell me was the way I would feel about love. He didn't manage to make me aware that I would struggle with anxieties when thinking about the injustices of society. He was unable to warn me how the education system would make me hate the thought of standing in a classroom to educate children, using a system set to keep them stuck in a society reminiscent of Big Brother or 1984, a surveillance state.

'Niyah Adenike, you are the one.' He would tell me. 'The Hand of God is upon you. The ancestors rejoiced at your birth.'

As a child, these words had me dancing. I floated around my house on cloud nine, not realising how disliked this made me within the family. I became the rotten fruit. I was frowned upon. My cousins treated me as though I had lesions upon my skin. My siblings rolled their eyes whenever I walked into a room with my crown upon my head. My aunts and uncles would shake their heads whenever I visited.

I was the void created from Papa's words. His love was an open wound prone to infection, hatred seeping in from my pathogenic relations that I had never noticed. I had never realised until I was seven years old, more aware of what the idea of love was to be. I may have noticed much earlier on, but seven was the particular age I remember being infected by this familial hatred.

* * *

There we were in the garden; music filled the air in the shape of a gazebo to prevent the sun rays from burning our skin, the smell of the chicken on the barbeque grill was hypnotic, and I had to hold my tummy to stop it from grumbling too loudly. But, on the other hand, the chatter and laughter from the adults were joyous to watch, and my cousins and siblings were carefree.

My heart was giddy. I wanted to play so badly and was scared to ask. My issue was this, I always had a book to read, except today. Today Mommy told me to leave the book at home.

'Niyah, you must play with your cousins.' I remember her saying.

How could I play with my cousins? I didn't know how to. It was always typical for me to cling to my mother or grandparents, but I knew today would be different. Papa would be doing the barbeque, and my Grandmother would be in the kitchen making drinks and finishing the rice and peas. Aunt Shirley would have already done the coleslaw, and Uncle Ron would have made an array drinks. Mommy would have already done the mac and cheese. The ladies would all be in the kitchen talking, and everyone knows that little children can't be in earshot of 'big people business' as they all love to call it. When it comes to the men, they would be playing dominoes and either drinking Red Stripe or Heineken.

'Niyah, you need to play with your cousins,' mum repeated to me as I looked at her with questioning eyes before we walked into the house of her parents.

I wanted to play because this is what my mother wanted, so I was giddy with nerves.

'What are you playing?' I asked with an accent I no longer remember how to summon. My question landed on deaf ears.

I ran up to Jah, my cousin, a year older than I am and asked again. This time, I plucked up a little more courage and put a smile on my face, only to be told 'no-one wants to play with you, Niyah', in a thick Southern American accent with a growl the did not hide very well underneath his tongue.

Suddenly, it's as though the music fell beneath my feet, and suddenly my skin set on fire. It made no sense why Jah said what he said, but I knew I felt hurt. I couldn't believe he had said that, so I had to ask why.

'Because no one likes you.' His eyes, a shade of pain, glowered at me. 'And I hate you.' He continued, this time, loud enough for Papa to hear.

That was it. That was all it took to break my spirit. That was all it took to break the family apart. Four words. The operative word, Hate.

'Boy, what kind of nonsense is that?' I remember Papa said as he wrapped his hand into a fist with Jah's shirt crumpled in it. Jah's face was filled with fear as Papa dragged him towards his torso.

Jah couldn't answer. He had nothing to say. Everyone around froze. The women rushed out of the kitchen, and his mum stood there. No one had ever seen Papa angry. I had never seen this man before, and I was petrified.

'Boy, answer my question! What you mean you hate your cousin?'

'I-I-I...'

'Puss have yuh tongue?' Papa looked Jah square in his eyes and told him to apologise to me, demanding that he apologised. My body was uncontrollable, and I shook like a leaf. Jah, on the other hand, had tears streaming down his cheeks. It's as though we were in a parallel world as I had no idea that boys were allowed to cry.

'But why yuh crying? Niyah should be the one crying! Stop your nonsense.' Now we were back to reality. Boys were not allowed to cry. Not the boys in my family. Not black boys.

Jah inhaled deeply, and with that, it was as though his tears disappeared.

He didn't apologise to me because his mother took him from her Father's grip and that was it. We didn't see them again. No more summer visits, and Christmas is just an ordinary day we spend together in separate houses.

* * *

The foundation of my family was shaken when I was seven. Over the years, I remember hearing my mother having arguments on the phone with other family members about that fateful day. The day I drove a wedge between her and her siblings, between *her* and *their* parents.

At school, I preferred to sit in a corner in the playground and read away. I withdrew from the friends I had. I would never try to talk to anyone in the class, and, as I got older, I became the victim of bullying. My curse followed me throughout primary school and followed me into secondary school. I spent nights with my face in the pillow, washing it with my tears. When it came to time for sixth form, I left Lewisham borough for Southwark. I chose to leave my past behind and venture into an area where no one knew me. Sixth form was where I met my best friend, Ayomide.

Never had I stopped to speak to my parents about it because I did not believe they would have understood. My siblings nor anyone else, for that matter, had ever really looked in my direction, and they all did their best to exclude me.

When I was old enough to have a mobile phone, I didn't have any of their numbers for several months. It wasn't until Mum had asked me to call Charlene, I revealed I didn't have it. Mum was shocked. We were all living under her roof, and she had no idea that her older children had excluded me. We are better now, but our relationship still has holes.

It's a funny thing with WhatsApp: your Grandparents get taught to use it, create a family group chat. Three to be precise; one just for their children, one for the grandchildren only, and another for the whole family. They send a message explicitly asking all of their Grandchildren to be present for a meeting at their house, with a date and time. No one can oblige.

We are now old enough to make decisions for ourselves, travel on our own. We couldn't use the excuse of waiting for our parents to drop us, depending on them to take us to our Grandparent's house.

They explicitly said that all of their grandchildren should be present for a meeting at their house, with a date and time, no room for excuses.

I guess they still felt guilty for what happened between Jah and me all those years ago. It's good that we have had the chance to discuss it as a family but, in my opinion, it's taken too long. This issue should have been resolved the minute it happened.

I guess where pride is involved, we must continue to live with the pain until it is removed.

I have learnt a lot from Ayomide and other friends I have made over the years regarding family relationships.

I have also been trying to rectify this idea that I am not worthy of anyone's love. Difficulties I have previously faced are nothing in comparison to this. To have been summoned to my Grandparents' house after 28 years to repair the damage done was a relief for me, about time.

I needed validation to help me to heal. I needed to hear from my cousin what his definition of hate meant and where he learnt it. I needed to have my siblings tell me that they were not particularly mad at me for anything I had done. I needed my grandparents to explain what they meant by saying I am unique and the key to change within the family. I needed not to feel victimised anymore.

I lost faith in love and, for many years, have found it difficult to open up to anyone who wanted to get close. It put me in situations where I was sleeping with a friend because I didn't want to commit. I went on dating sites hoping that those conversations would drive me to feel a particular way about a guy and allow him to get close to me. I was not too fond of couples to a degree because I wanted what they had and wasn't able to allow myself to find it. I want children but am yet to settle into a relationship. I fear that my children would receive the butt end of the impartiality I have received over the years. It's not right to bring a child into that, is it?

This meeting was needed for me.

It was the trigger for my journey of understanding love within the black community, the black home, black relationships, and within the black self.

Our history didn't begin with slavery, but our lack of understanding of black love truly did.

Now I am to make changes within myself to impact others. I work with families from minority backgrounds, so eloquently put, those from deprived areas. I want to help them to heal. However, this isn't possible if I cannot move on from the summer of 1991. I can't keep those ghosts dancing around me when I walk into rooms. I cannot look into the eyes of a mother and tell her to wake up if I am still embracing the slumber which has rocked me gently into frequent nightmares.

I've never seen the stars fight, but my people do. My people look into each other's souls, staring deep within, yet can still murder each other, physically and verbally. This is what I want to help to prevent. I want to help to decrease the crime rate in Lewisham. I want to help young people to come to terms with what love is, what love should truly be to them and not the fictitious feuds or the unfavoured acts they must carry out to prove they love or are loyal.

If the stars were to fight
Would we be stabbed each night
With a dagger of a fragmented point
As it crashed to the Earth
After being hit with such force
Where hatred was its ruler?

If the stars were to fight
Would the Moon cry each night
And lose her glow
Knowing the Sun would need to
Shed pieces of himself to replace
Wonders for the night sky?

If the stars were to fight
Would we be happy people
Knowing the universe is such a dystopian place
Unable to be at peace
With the pains we've been through
Settling our slave syndromes
That we could sleep easily?

If the stars were to fight
Would we be happy people

Knowing the universe is such a dystopian place
Unable to be at peace
With the pains we've been through
Settling our slave syndromes
That we could sleep easily?

If the stars were to fight
Would the black nation be one
No longer burying bodies
One after the other
Leaving no mother with dry eyes
With no news of another
Lost to knife crime?

Why can we not be like the stars
They who watch over us at night
They who reside peacefully
Dancing with each other at midnight
Entertaining the moon
Keeping each other company?

They do not fight.
So why do we?
I do not think I would have ever thought of these words had it not been for my family. I have now printed copies to hand to my families so that they may have something to remind them that if we are to be as precious and beautiful as stars, we cannot afford to fight amongst ourselves.

It is relatively dangerous when individuals are unaware of their worth. We diminish ourselves when unable to see the greatness we have caught beneath our wings.

When I think of the disrespect we show to ourselves, it makes me wonder what life would have been like for us all if slavery had not occurred. What would England look like? Would an African country host the leader of the Free World? Would African Royalty hold greater power than The British Royal Family? Had Africa been the most powerful continent, would we, as blacks, as Moors, hold ourselves in greater esteem?

These questions, as provocative as they are, are the root of some of my frustrations. However, as I know these questions will never be answered, they push me into wanting more for us. I want more for the blacks in my community. I want more for my family. I would love for my sown seeds to marry themselves to the knowledge that says they are greater than they have ever perceived themselves to have been.

Well, Orion, it's goodnight from me. I have an early start tomorrow and need to be able to remain awake for my clients.

With purpose, I'm signing that my crown is cherished.

Niyah Adenike Thomas.

Friday 26th July 2019 ~~Friday 26th July 2019~~ Friday 26th July 2019

Dear Orion,

Being at home is the best feeling ever. I got in, and the first thing I wanted to do was to throw my clothes all over the place.

Today seemed more stressful than I expected it to be. Getting to work and being thrown into the deep end with a new family who had already been seeing another worker threw me off course.

Yes, I know I am to embrace change. However, to open an email sent late last night at 11:33 pm with a 12-page document I'm expected to digest for a 9:00 am appointment just 30 minutes before this time is not the change I want to embrace—all on a Friday morning, to be precise.

I love my Fridays to begin as my Mondays do, slow and relaxed with a mug of steaming hot coffee on my desk which takes me at least 20 minutes to get through. Whilst blowing my way through my coffee, I add some ambience with either tranquil zen music or morning jazz, depending on my mood.

This ritual of mine I do as I open emails and trawl through them, then I give myself some time to do my deep breathing. Is that not the perfect way to begin and end working weeks? I thought so. Nevertheless, managers and co-workers thought it best to alter my Friday morning routine, unbeknownst to me.

With my day starting like that, it's as though everything else went haywire. My families today were very unsettled. My mind was not there. I was present but seemed to have been having an out-of-body experience.

Now that the workday is over, I feel selfish; I hadn't given my families the time they truly needed. I was so wrapped up in my inability to have complete control over the routine I set for myself, instead of being present and giving them all of me, spending the time listening to them and talking through their circumstances. Though I am not their family member, we share the same coding for skin colour within our cells. I should have paid more attention, but, have always been told that I shouldn't cry over spilt milk. I do hope that for whatever reason this had occurred, it was a good one.

Thinking it over, I saw a family who was similar to one of mine today—a married couple with three toddlers; two boys and one girl. The parents looked as though they were in their mid-thirties, as with my family. The resemblance between the parents was so uncanny. Dad, the household joker. Mum, the calm. The difference is how they parent their children and work together, knowing their dissimilarities as individuals.

The family I work with, let's call them the Agyepongs, are a Ghanaian family. They tend to clash due to cultural differences. Weird that, right? Culturally different, yet their heritage is the same. Their parents raised them in different cultures; Dad, a first-generation immigrant and Mum, a third-generation immigrant. Where Dad is used to mothers being the disciplinarians for the toddlers, Mum feels it should be his responsibility to show that he is the man of the house.

It isn't easy to know what to say to them as I do not want to offend either of their beliefs, but I see the impact it has on their children. The Agyepongs are nothing like my other families. Like those of the family I saw today, their children are polite and do not cause as much havoc in the room as other children would.

I see that the Agyepongs do love each other, though they fear that they are drifting apart, I have been told on occasions by each of them separately. Though frustrated with each other, every time they look at one another, it's as though sparks begin to fly. This is the love I saw between the couple today. I've seen them on several occasions, and as with the Agyepongs, they have never exchanged an unkind word or bitter look.

I do feel, however, that the Agyepongs have regretted having children as they couldn't see these turbulent times ahead of them. It's now for us to work towards them sharing their love for each other with their children, dispelling the lessons they learned from their parents and thinking of strategies to make their children's childhood stable, fun, and, most importantly, healthy.

What I would love for the Agyepongs is that they would morph into a similar version of their lookalikes. Hopefully, they would empower other families who see them. I want them to impact single black women such as myself, give them hope that there are black men out there for them, who are capable of loving her and the children she will give birth to for him. I want them to show single black men that it doesn't have to be difficult in relationships with black women.

> If you've never seen them
> It could simply mean they are at home
> Teaching their young royals
> About their importance.
>
> A lot more of their presence
> Would be the light many of us seek
> But they too must have the opportunity
> To embrace their privacy.
>
> We can't depend on them
> To be the definition of love
> But must take what is displayed,
> Deep, pure love.

I wonder if outsiders have ever viewed my family in this light? Has anyone ever stopped long enough to look at my parents to perceive the fountain of adoration in their eyes? Did they look at my siblings and me to see that our parents were doing the best they could for us?

If there had been someone to have stepped into our lives to help us to try to fix our lives, I don't know how my family would have responded to it. My grandparents are devoted to this Jamaican kind of pride, which means no outsider can come and tell them what to do to make their household life work. They believe that their way is the right way.

This has also been passed down to my mother and her siblings. There is no way under the sun that she will allow any of her siblings to tell her how to raise us. And my mother cannot let her siblings see that she has an essay in return about their parenting styles.

This is our issue and I don't blame them for their thought patterns. It all goes back to slavery and how our ancestors were taught to deal with each other. What didn't help was that we were still treated with the least regard; attacks were being made on us and we were still at risk of death. This led to parents overcompensating when it came to parenting their children. Their parenting styles came from fear of their child being targeted and not making it home.

Unlike the Jews who have had the world's support to speak about their traumas, blacks were always told to take a seat and get over it because it happened so many years ago. Both situations resulted in generational trauma. Nevertheless, when your trauma is put on the backburner because it is seen to have little importance, it forces you to bottle your pains, say nothing to anyone, and pass your toxicity onto your children.

We are from a culture where speaking up about that

thing which no longer occurs, thus doesn't directly bother you is forbidden. Dare you say the forbidden S-word, you become the condemned one in the home.

Now do you see where mental health comes into play in our households? This becomes cyclical. Parents parent based on how they were parented. Some cycles are broken because someone sees beyond the here and now, thinks about their upbringing and compares it to how they want their child to feel whilst growing up. No matter how hard we try, unless we parent according to our children's characteristics as well as choosing from the parenting we learnt growing up, and the changes in society, it will still be difficult. Unfortunately, it may result in our children still having difficulties growing up and struggling with their mental health.

It is important that no matter what we do, our children remember that we love them. It is important we not only say it to them, but show it through our actions too. These actions don't need to be linked with the buying of materialistic possessions. Instead, let it be about spending quality time together.

We've been poisoned in thinking that it is important to buy someone else's love instead of paying in quality time, investing that money lost on something which is either thrown away or misplaced. I want to make these changes when I have children. I do not want my child to be excluded from friendship groups as I was, or hated by their cousins. This is what I mean about parents parenting based on how they were parented. I've seen what it's like to be the favourite child or grandchild. That favouritism is what drove a wedge between my family members.

I want to help the families I work with to cultivate a mindset of equality amongst their children. I want for the parents to really dig deep within themselves, to find what it is that they do not want to repeat and what points they could take away and repeat in their parenting. I want them to know their children well enough to be able to discipline them accordingly. Parenting should have a holistic approach instead of fragmented; responding and reacting to the child based on what they have done such as praising and rewarding them, or reprimanding them when necessary.

Think I have to stop here. I am exhausted but I want to lay in the bath for a bit before my pre-sleep meditation.

With purpose, I'm signing that my crown is cherished.

Niyah Adenike Thomas.

Dear Orion,

'Sometimes your energy is off init. Like, you're all over the place and it's a lot. It's like you don't even know yourself.' Can you believe a friend actually said this to me? When we had this conversation, I called him a friend. Now, I don't call him. It was something in the way he said it which made me uncomfortable.

There was no love in his tone of voice. His energy felt dark. I felt lost as we spoke as I couldn't make sense of what was going on. Well, I did. I needed someone to speak to and he was that person I felt I could confide in. I called and explained how I was feeling and why, but somehow, he carefully made me feel as though I was the perpetrator.

I lost my trust in him after that conversation, especially having had a conversation with one of the girls who let me in on a little secret about him. The bigger part of this little secret, he was practically telling me that his energy is at times off and he doesn't know himself.

Friends are like leaves, if we consider ourselves to be trees. Some, the leaves of evergreen trees, others, the leaves of deciduous trees. Well, when I put it that way, I only have to think that makes us the trees, evergreen and deciduous. The type of tree we are, is related to the energies we pick up from our friends and how we react to it. We either keep them around because of the warmth they exude, or we side step our way out of their lives.

I hope that makes sense. My mind got away from me, but I believe that my explanation has a philosophical touch to it. Sometimes I like to sound extremely knowledgeable and it does come off well. I hope this is one of those moments.

What I truly wanted to convey was the idea that friends come and go. In time, some return, whilst others vanish, never to be seen again. I guess we can change my simile and say, some friends are like frisbees, others, boomerangs. Hmm, I like the idea of that, but I think I'll stick to trees.

It's as they say; some people are for a season, Sakura, and some are for a lifetime, Leyland Cypress. Sakura, most commonly known as the cherry blossom here in the UK, are spring trees. The blossoms are beautiful and the trees are glorious when decorated in these magnificent blooms. Once the trees undress themselves, that's it, you don't get to enjoy the beauty of it again until the following Spring. Leyland Cypress grows fast, is strong, and when grown close together in rows, they are perfect for screening wind, snow, and noise.

Our Sakura friends make us happy when they are blossoming. We love them for their blossoms that soften our hearts and minds. We, so mesmerised by their beauty, forget how fickle they are, even when they have fallen from their branches. The fact that their core is still there means once they unfold again, it will be someone else who their beauty will hypnotise.

Our Leyland Cypress friends are the ones who are there for us through thick and thin. They protect us from life's pains and, they shelter us when in need. Though we appreciate them, sometimes we forget that they are here to stay. It isn't until we step away from their shelter and protection, we realise how beneficial they are to us. The sense of feeling lost without them troubles us, but it's something we are unable to fathom until we are realigned with them.

In all of that, I am quite certain that I have more Sakura than Leyland Cypresses as friends. It is expected and no-one can say otherwise. My childhood was spent in the isolation I created. I found it difficult to open up to others which meant no-one hung around long enough to know the quirky side of me as well as the nerdy side. The teary side, as well as the strong-willed heart.

What made it more difficult was that I've never really known myself. Where I've spent a lifetime with my head trapped in fantasy worlds, I lost my truth and became a chameleon of characters. This is exactly what happened to me. I've been a dancer, a painter, a homeless person, a witch, and even a fairy. I've been married on countless occasions while trying to stay alive. I was completely unaware that I was alive in the wrong world.

We have found 'moods' in memes,
Lost in worlds created by others to satisfy our lack.
Lacking the understanding that happiness was never lost.

How we see ourselves
Isn't to do with our minds,
But more of their views.

Viewing the world as a detrimental landscape,
Escaping realities,
Trapping our minds within this cage of a body.

Maya figured out why the caged bird sung
And Alicia understood it too,
But there is much more than receiving a reason
If we aren't able to grasp it for us.

Instagram can guide us so far along
As we tread along the thinnest routes
Trying to better ourselves,

But we can't fill our bellies on short snippets
If we spend no time to introspect,
Yet we expect others to respect us
But we haven't got that self-discipline.

Implementing intrepid instances in inaugural
Neural notions notifying negligent
Times. Training thoughts to track
Rituals relating rightfully to routes
Of oneirism.
Spectacularly spectating situations of
self-destruction and self-actualisation
Prompting perfectly imperfect powers
Elevating emotions, entertaining energies
Correcting confidence uncovering creations
Taking time to talk to you.

We've become dependents of dependency
Seeking validation from them is a tendency
Needing them as guides
Submissive as brides
Losing trust in ourselves
is natural complacency.
This lack of understanding when it comes to
self-examination
Causes us to mindlessly point fingers
It's never a case of ready aim fire
But instead shoot now and come to realisation
later
Just like black bodies dropping like flies
At the pull of a police's trigger
We act now and think later.

But what if we trained the mind
As much as we did bodies

Taught it how to pause as we do our fingers for
Netflix
Would it not mean we'd take the blame for our
actions
Without becoming compulsive accusers?

Don't we all do this,
Tell friends and family, they are in control of
their actions
If another being does something they do not
agree with?
Don't we tell them to deal with their own inse-
curities
And try not to project?
But for some God forsaken reason, we can't
seem to take our own advice.
Is it truly null and void when it becomes per-
sonal?

Personifying our thoughts,
Placing them in host bodies.
Must we see them in someone else
To be able to identify that it's wrong?
That we are wrong,
And by wrapping them around someone else,
We detach
Hoping they become better people
Not realising it is ourselves we are to have the
issue with
It is us who needs fixing.

Let's correct ourselves here and now.
How we see ourselves
Isn't to do with their minds
But more of our views.

Our views of ourselves
We need to become one with who we are now
Look at who we were then
And figure out who we want to be tomorrow.

That way, we'll no longer be dependents of dependency
Seeking validation from them shouldn't be a tendency
We shouldn't need them as guides
To submit as brides
And no longer should we trust in ourselves
To be in complacency.

Okay, I think I can now agree with what my friend had said about not knowing myself. I'm still figuring myself out, but who really knows themselves? To figure me out, I've been going on dates. Somewhere in my mind, by meeting and getting to interact with these men, I would get to know what I like and what I don't like about guys. It means I know what to look out for when I want to settle down and get married.

I will let you know more about the dates, I promise. I want to share with you the other methods I've been testing out. I've been going to art galleries, experimented with smoking, tried to drink enough alcohol to have a good time, go to the cinema, go to the theatre and entertain a certain idea. Next up on 'In the Life of Niyah Adenike Thomas' right? Ha! Everything I've been doing, I've done with my Leyland Cypress, Ayomide and some other friends I'll tell you about later as well.

It has been fun and scary at times, just being out of my comfort zone. As I have been out more, I'm seeing through friends and I can tell there is something different about them, or maybe it is me who is different, changing and growing. Ayomide tells me this, in her words, 'Niyah, your walk has changed' but she has never explained what she means. But I have only guessed that she means I have been growing, and it shows in my walk. It was her who taught me the art of meditation. Not only have I been calm and at peace at the end, but I have come out of it with a greater insight. This insight says it is now time for me to.

With purpose, I'm signing that my crown is cherished.

Niyah Adenike Thomas.

Dear Orion,

Today's entry is very personal. Extremely personal.

I will be introducing you to my body.

I've come to realise that I don't quite like my body. I do not spend the time looking in the mirror at my naked self, so all my truth comes from a covered body.

Upon discovering such a shocking truth, I stood before my reflection today and slowly stripped. My black body was a foreign language. She spoke softly, but reprimanded me.

I ran my hands over my breasts, intrigued by the spots I owned. Lifting them separately, I felt how heavy they truly are. They aren't small, something I have always known, hence my jealousy of every woman with membership to the Itty Bitty Titty Community. Not that it's a bad thing, but for some reason it's always felt like a shame.

I turned it into a bad thing without good reason.

I was shocked at how fair my torso is in complexion when compared to my arms and my face. At that point, I decided I must wear more bikinis on holiday. I'd love to have a darker complexion, not as a fetish but because I think deep rich melanin is outstandingly beautiful; unfortunately, I've not always had this outlook, but I'll tell you about it later. It's not that I hate my coffee skin, I'm just not in love with it.

I want to be able to parade around in love, strutting as though my body is my own. Instead, I have her covered as best and as often as possible

With my thoughts on re-run, a tap in my tear ducts opened drowning my eyes in tears. The lack of confidence I have in myself made me feel ashamed of how I have treated my body. This is something I know I need to rectify and readjust.

I know I'll get there though. I will get to the day I can hold my head high and be comfortable as a black Queen.

With purpose, I'm signing that my crown is cherished.

Niyah Adenike Thomas

Royalty was given to me the day my creation began.

Confession #1:

I am a recipient of a certain kind of benefit.
We've seen each other in lights.
Not as bright as the sun
Or as dim as the moon.
Guided by LEDs and ecstasy,
Our bodies are melodically divine
With the wrong form of divinity
And lust is just a mere mortal thing.
We are led by a subconscious model of needs.

Dear Orion,

I have to honestly get it off my chest tonight. Last night was about introspection, and tonight a secret which will weigh heavily if not put out there. That idea I have been entertaining is a recent thing. I can't believe it's happening.

There's a friend I have who I can't say I ever looked at beyond seeing them as a being with whom I share this planet. Our relationship is formed on the basis that we share laughter over the silliest things. Though we have this, I had never thought about what his body looks like beneath his clothing, so it was natural for me to have been shocked when he messaged to suggest that this ordeal, of sex without attachment, could happen... If I had any interest that was.

I remember frantically, yet voicelessly exclaiming at my phone when I received the message:
'Whenever you're ready shout me yeah.
For the booty call'.
How does a woman preserving herself for true love respond to such a message? Booty call?

My main thought at the time was, 'really Kyron?'

See, Kyron was attractive, but not my version of drop dead gorgeous. His face was the definition of a psychologically attractive face, simple and symmetrical. He is of light complexion; some people from the Caribbean would call him red, or maybe that's just Jamaicans. Here in England, he's a lightie. To me, he is just Kyron. Ky to be short.

He is tall, taller than I am, and slim. His eyes, I think, are brown. His lips, not too full, but not too empty. He is not someone I've ever analysed. He's just... Kyron.

So, this is why that message had me freaking out. It sent neurons flying. I was energised. Excited. I've felt so invisible for a long time. Guys have never been my strongest point. To have a small friendship group, I find it much more challenging to interact and get to know guys. But there was something about Kyron. He was easy to talk to when we met. Now we are at this point where he has sent me that message. I've felt invisible for such a long time and it made me feel good to be seen by someone. Even if that someone is Kyron.

Kyron sees me. At least, I think he does.

But morals. My morals. I didn't know how to interact with booty calls. Couldn't tell if it was correct and whether I was to entertain it. I have always pictured myself to be a Proverbs 31 kind of woman. Precious. Virtuous. Clothed with dignity. Owner of wise words. Faithful. Honourable.

Am I these things if I lay with a man who has no intention of marrying me? I know his intentions are laid in a bed of sex, but is he only sexually attracted to me? Is he even in any way attracted to me? Of all the women in London, why me?

I expected nothing more than the out of body, out of mind experience with him.

How will this affect me when getting into relationships? I won't be able to date if my time is spent behind closed doors with him, will I?

I still go about normal routines and only see him on days I have no other plans, or when I choose to change my plans last minute. So, I guess I don't need to worry about being able to meet someone else. Do I?

I don't know if he is a seasonal friend, but this has been going on for some months now.

I was on a journey trying to understand love. Specifically love between blacks. My love. Self-love. Now, I feel I've already failed. It feels good to be in this, but I almost feel as though I'm essentially cheating on me, Niyah Adenike Thomas.

Niyah, before Kyron, is a 35 year old prude who does everything by the book. She cares for her body; no smoking, attempted rare drinking, no drugs. Yes, like everyone else, even vegans, she eats junk food. She enjoys chocolate, especially during PMS. She is a humanitarian and despises idiots and their mindset.

Niyah, before Kyron, hates travelling on public transport, yet she does it because she has no other option. She can't stomach the sight of blood, so tries to stay as far away from hospitals as she possibly can. She is very competitive so hates any activity which requires her to be a good sportsman. However, she enjoys the thrill of playing tennis and goes to her local tennis club up to three, maybe four times a week.

Why do I therefore crave Kyron's attention or the feel of him against my skin?

I have been doing well on my own for the last three years. No men. No dating. And definitely NO SEX. I was doing well. By not having a man in my life, I was able to focus on my career. By not dating, I wasn't spending my time on someone who didn't deserve it, in turn, my energy remained intact. And with not having sex, it meant I wasn't opening myself to every demon out there.

But something draws me to Kyron.

Whatever it is, I need to figure it out before it consumes me.

As a woman who places her morals before yielding to temptations, I am seen as the sensible one in my group of girlfriends. I know if my parents were to catch wind of my thoughts they would show how disappointed they are.

Though I am past the approval of my parents when it comes to the man I'm giving access to my body, it's still important that they approve of the man I will choose to build a home with. And no Orion, that man will not be Kyron.

What else should I do? He and I have an agreement albeit unhealthy for us both, however, for now, it is satisfying. Well, I need to figure things out. Do I want to continue Being Mary Jane? Or do I want something deeper than the as and when casualness of it all to put my heart in harm's way?

I'm going to say goodnight to you now Orion. I know I've given you a lot to digest.

We've diverted our attention
Averted our love
Given room to toxins
Pressed flowers against noses
For disappointments from failed expectations
To harm us

Shop bought stress and
Second hand damage
Shakes its way throughout our core
Now we question if Black Love exists
In skins richly melanated.
With purpose, I'm signing that my crown is cherished.

Niyah Adenike Thomas.

<u>Tuesday 30th July 2019</u>

Dear Orion,

I met the most egoistic man today. Mortgage advisor. Owns 4 houses, rents 3, of which 1 is in America and one, Jamaica. He is originally from America, came to live in the UK at the age of 25 for a new life. He has 2 children whom he never sees because supposedly the Mum won't allow him permission to see them. He has a BMW. Never really liked the idea of having pets. He only has a house in Jamaica because he wants the money from tourists, so his house is in Negril. He is a middle child of 3. He grew up in a very strict house and was constantly sneaking out. He tried cannabis once, but didn't like the taste of it. His favourite drink is Courvoisier. He only likes going out for meals, and is not a big fan of dancing.

He has always chosen poorly when it comes to women. His last girlfriend was a big talker and he found he could never get a word in. I can understand his frustration because he had not shut up since we met. As well as being a big talker, she turned him down when he wanted to have sex and that was a big no-no. Guess I can take from that, women must always want to have sex with him.

I was bored.

We spent at least 3 hours together and, in between the claps of his mouth as he ate and the flapping of his gum as he told me his life's biography, I couldn't get a word in. To sit and listen to everything he said, I almost felt as though he was preaching at me. Saying that, he did actually begin to preach at me. Weird. How can you tell me about wanting to be a good Christian when you want to sleep with women before marriage? I really wanted to ask him about the scripture in the Bible which says that you can have sex before you are wed.

This man, though handsome, had a mind not to be explored. I love getting to know about people, it intrigues me, but his self-adoration was nothing that caught my eyes. He didn't hold my heart, nor did he keep my interest. I spent more time looking at my phone hoping that it was time for me to call it quits, than I in the end spent listening to him.

If he were to be asked any questions about me, he would not even be able to say what my name was, yet I can answer many things about him. His name? Quincy Pierre Patrick. His birthday? 22nd August 1981. His favourite colour? The orange hue during sunset. His favourite meal? Thanksgiving. Can you even say that's a meal?

This guy has been nonstop interested in himself.

We met on Hinge. Out of boredom, and in hopes someone came along, I set up an account. He was one of my matches. There, our conversations were good. He entertained me, I think I entertained him. He was seemingly interested. I was genuinely interested. I can assume I made him laugh, he honestly made me laugh. We were a perfect fit.

So I thought.

I didn't think I would have ever met anyone like him. I thought I was a good judge of character, but when one hasn't had the opportunity to interact with many people growing up, I guess we don't learn how to judge people well enough.

I wish I understood men,
Hoping they would give me a sign,
Not wanting to get too close,
Knowing I'd be devoured by their attitudes.
I need help.
To be guided by a light form of some sort.

I've only ever enjoyed the all sorts kind of sort

When it comes to sweets, not men.
I need help.
Only stars have given me the needed kind of
sign.
I knew I needed new signs for new attitudes.
I've found my heart hurts not being close.

But I've found myself being too close.
One of the troubles through which I've had to
sort,
I need words to help with my attitudes.
It's never easy when it comes to these men.
I need an object, a gesture, a name, a number, a
sign,
I need help.

Help
I'm not close enough but I'm too close.
I've seen enough people twirling the same sign,
A word, formulated when that trouble is its own
sort
And it cannot be compared to that associated
with men,
Not when it comes to comparing attitudes.

These obscure, undeniable attitudes
Have caused me nothing but pain, help.
I thought I would have loved, but God, these
men.
Their energies when in proximities too close
Forces me to reserve my being as I, through
everything, sort,
As I climb on table tops looking for a sign.
Just a simple sign.

Help me amend my attitudes.
I'm done with this OCD, needing to,
every aspect of my life, sort.
Not by colours, shapes or sizes, help.
I now need to find someone to whom I can be
close,
I need to pick at least one of these men.

This prayer has asked for nothing but a small
sign just for me to get the help,
To work my way through these attitudes just to
be, to them, close
As with clothes and cupboards, I want to sort
through these men.

It's been difficult to write that. Now that I have, I can only say I do feel lighter. To know that the need, or want, to be able to curl up in the arms of a man has been so problematic because I have one mindset is traumatic on its own accord.

I wouldn't say I have daddy issues, but there is something preventing me from settling down. It's something that has cropped up in the past but I ignored it.

Now, hello monster.

They say to heal yourself you must come to a realisation that you are not your past. I wouldn't say I've thought myself to be my past, but it has played a huge role in my present. Another thing about healing, something I've seen floating around on the internet which is very thought provoking is the idea that healing requires one to let go of emotions, energy, and mindsets. A very big ask.

The two do marry well. Well, the idea of realisation goes well with the art of letting go. It's just for you to realise this means you must accept what's happened. Do not mistake what I've said to mean that you were deserving of what happened to you. To accept, you must revisit and to revisit is painful.

This pain blocks true happiness. A pain which forces you into denial throws you into a well of unhealthy habits which produces desperate happiness. I don't know if there is any research to prove this, but it's exactly what happened to me. Come to think of it, I'm sure there is certainly, someone out there will have a big but about this, however, it doesn't bother me.

I've overcome the pain, accepted that it's there and will always be a reminder of the past. As I'm now writing, I have to agree, you do have to understand that you are not your past. Once you do this, you will, in time, be able to move forward with greater confidence and really walk in more power.

My pain is universal and sits beneath many floorboards. Some families are communities willing to confront it, while others continue to build lives around it. I do wonder if this happens in the black communities because we had no-one to fight for us during slavery. I've read that though circumstantial, there is a name for it: epigenetics. This notion of trauma attaches itself to genes, making its way through generations. I'd boldly raise my hand to say this is learned behaviour.

Our ancestors were taught that these foul behaviours, though wrong, were unpunishable and okay to happen. I wasn't there when these heinous events happened, of course, but with what I've studied, I'm sure they would have been beaten for speaking out.

That's how I felt when it happened.

* * *

'Niyah, if you do it, we'll play with you.' Ricardo said as he put his arm around me. I was desperate to be included, but something felt wrong.

'I-I don't think we're meant to.' I hesitantly replied.

It had been a little over 3 months since things went wrong at our grandparents' house. I don't recall what Mommy said, but there was a good reason, as she had put it, for us to be here.

'You want to play with us don't you?' I nodded my head, afraid to speak.

'So?' He looked at me with hopeful eyes. 'Are you going to do it?'

'Are you going to like me?' My voice quivered. 'Jah said no-one likes me.'

'We will like you and play with you.'

Ricardo was 9 years old and I looked up to him. Though Jah told me they didn't like me, I still looked up to my older cousins.

I believed him.

I allowed him. Gave him permission by simply nodding my head.

He touched me and to my dismay told me, 'you don't have anything there.'

'Yes I do!' I quickly responded. I didn't know what Ricardo was talking about but I knew I had those two little bumps on my chest. My nipples were where he touched.

He touched me again, searching for what I knew was not missing. At least, that's what I thought. This time around, his hand lingered that bit longer. He found my nipples, face scrunched, he was disappointed. I could tell. I just didn't know why. He removed his hands, shrugged his shoulders and told me to follow him.

I felt a little butterfly dance in my stomach. Her wings tickled the lining of my walls and excitement grew. For the first time, despite what Jah said, my cousin was happy to play with me.

We headed into his room while the adults remained downstairs and uur other cousins were in his older brother's room. I had never been to his room before.

Something was different about today. When we got to my aunt's house, my Mother sent me upstairs as soon as my grandparents arrived. On a normal day, I would have been able to sit with my Mum; with a book in my hand, I would have sat at her feet.

Today was different.

I was nervous when I got to the top of the stairs. I sat there, armed with my book in hand. Ricardo spotted me and got me talking to him, now here we were. His room.

His room was similar to my brother's. A football motif took precedence. The wall by his bed was occupied by a Manchester United wallpaper, the other walls were a solid red decorated with posters of footballers. On his desk, a small Jamaican flag, not so similar to my brother's. My brother Nick had a big Jamaican flag on his wall.

Ricardo's desk sat underneath his bed. He had a study bunk bed with a desk and drawers beneath it. Just like Nick's.

The butterfly in me grew into a tornado of fear. Though I allowed his hands to rest on my undeveloped breasts, it made no sense as to why it was just the two of us in his room to play. I thought we would have gone to David's room with the others.

'Come in and close the door then.' His frustration cloaked the hush of his voice. My feet heavy, stuttered as I stepped forward. The air, clogging my airways with panic, yet my feet continued.

'I thought-' I paused. Swallowing the air which was caught in my throat. 'I thought we were going to play with everyone else.'

'Yeah, after'.

'After what?' My voice sounded different in my ear. It was no longer afraid.

He stepped towards me and quickly pecked me on my lips. Confusion caused my hands to push him away.

I wanted to run, but I think my legs were replaced with Jell-O. I thought I would have fallen over had I moved.

'You have to do what I say before you get to play with everybody else.'

'I don't want to kiss you though.'

'Just do it and everything else that I say.'

'No.' I sounded much bolder than I felt. Mentally, I had already turned to open the door. Physically I was frozen with fear.

'You have to.' He demanded my small frame.

My mind, blank. I looked past him. He became a shadow of himself. His chocolate skin burnt by the fear which stung my eyes.

We kissed. He fondled the space between my legs. We kissed some more and he placed my hand on something small between his legs. And once more we kissed.

The start of many nights of our meetings. This was our doll-house. We didn't play dress-up, but over the years, we became very acquainted with stripping.

She flaps her wings continuously
Figure 8 allows her to hover
But that infinity chain was broken
Now she struggles to be in a better place

She sinks into bed
Covered by the quilt whose stitches
Aren't as closely knitted as they are
And their small frames rise and fall simultaneously.

7-9-11
Her hummingbird days were meant to be simple
7-9-11

Her hummingbird days were meant to be easy
7-9-11
Her hummingbird days were meant to be innocent

Yet the simplicity she needed
Became complicated.
She wasn't protected by their structures
Their bloodline
Their links
Nothing protected her
And instead,
She became the home of secrets.

Her heart heavy with burdens
She remembers everything she was unable to
forget.

The ease at which she was to develop
Became difficulties.
She had to keep the touches to herself
As fear ruled her life
She didn't want to be found out
But she knew it wasn't right
Yet her mouth has been kept shut.

Her heart heavy with burdens
She remembers everything she was unable to
forget.

Her innocence died
That first night they were covered under that
quilt.
To think their blood was meant to save her,
His hands touched her vagina

Her hands were guided to his penis
Now she will always remember
The very first time her hands
Touched a member of a male.

Her heart heavy with burdens
She remembers everything she was unable to forget.

She was 7-9-and-11 years old
Now
Guilt-hurt-shame
Chokes her soul and those days her mum said
'Would you tell me if you were raped?'
She lied, said yes,
Yet inside she wanted to
Curl into her mother's arm
And tell her about the nights
They were under the quilt
When he would place his hands over her body
Or guide her hands over his
And she can't even remember
If he had ever penetrated her.

There were times after she forgave him
She'd be on the phone to him
Trying to get over it
But he had the nerve to ask
Who the guys were that she was with.
She wanted to tell him
'You have no right to pretend to care
For you lost that opportunity when I was
7
9
11 years old.'

He was the reason her heart was so cold
She hated men because her cousin abused her
But he may not have noticed because
He was 8-10-12
Evenly rounded but not mentally grounded
He stole her simple life
Her easy days
Her innocent heart.

'I wonder if he remembers that he ruined me?'

She bottled it up for many years
And it wasn't until she was 22
Away from home
Slumped against her wall
Tattered and torn
On the phone she told her mum the truth
Her words scratching her mum's eardrums

'I believed he did it to her.
He touched her the way he touched me
I didn't know how to tell you
And now I wish I had done years ago
But I don't know
I just couldn't do it
I know it was wrong

But mum, I didn't want to hurt you.
It wasn't until I was in year 7
I accidentally said to some friends
That I kissed my cousin.
It was the looks they gave me
Which knocked sense into me
I was ashamed and
The guilt-hurt-shame

Took over me.'

Her mother couldn't believe what she heard
Her daughter hid these things from her for
years.
Her sister's son
Took advantage of her daughter
Now her daughter has to live
With the memories she was unable to forget.

But now she feels free
And has returned to
The hummingbird she used to be.
But the sureness that she's forgiven him
Completely
Isn't necessarily a hundred percent.

She was 7-9-11
Molested by her cousin
He was 8-10-12
Trapped her under the quilt
Incest lingering between the sheets
She wasn't the beautiful hummingbird
She was meant to be
Not for more than 6 years of her life.
It's a shame I had to go through that, but it has helped
with my growth. Yes, I was burdened by it for years after
I came to terms with the danger I was in. I began to use
it as a reason for becoming detached. Guys became ob-
jects. I used them until I was bored. None meant anything
to me.

So no, I do not have daddy issues. I have cousin issues.
I have incest issues. I couldn't understand how these
chain of events were linked to the meaning of my name.

I was alone in a world where family was not the thread

which held an individual together. Family tore me apart.
I think it's now time for me to cleanse before I sleep.
Having awoken my inner child and thrown many memo-
ries and emotions at her, she is now as tired as I am.
I will leave it here for tonight.

With purpose, I'm signing that my crown is cherished.

Niyah Adenike Thomas.

Realisation No. 1:
My Mental Is Indescribably Important
#MMIII

Wednesday 31st July 2019

Dear Orion,

I couldn't go to work today. Having unearthed such troubles last night, I spent hours crying before I slept. I knew I wouldn't be able to face my colleagues let alone my clients. At times like this I felt as though I was a hypocrite when working with other families to either help them out of their dysfunction, or help to save them from heading into dysfunction, when I myself am from dysfunction. On the surface, my family looks strong and well-kept together, when in reality, my family is far from perfect. I at times, judging the situation, am open with the families to whom I've been assigned. I inform them of some of the difficulties that I have faced within and how it could have been prevented had my parents had better control, had they understood what self-love truly was, to then pass on to us.

I arranged 10 of my candles along the bathroom floor, mindfully lighting each. One by one, I allowed their flames to dance, to flicker gracefully in hopes my cells could join in with their laughter. Listening to the water as it flowed from tap to bath, I added lavender oil and Epsom salt to it. The smell lifted my spirit. Aromatherapy along with water therapy, no better way to rejuvenate in my opinion.

As I immersed myself in the water, I suddenly felt overwhelmed once again. The beginning of my healing process. My tears flowed as though my body was recycling the water in which I laid. I always thought I had fully recovered, but there seems to be areas of me which seem to always be ready to erupt. It took years for me to be honest with my parents, but I have yet to confront my cousin.

There is still a strain on my family, though the relationship between my siblings and I is much better. Just by getting older, we learned to communicate with each other though there still were animosities between us. It wasn't until we went to our grandparents house, the first of supposedly more family bonding, we got together as siblings to have a discussion which was nothing short of needed. Additionally, the relationship between myself and my cousins is getting better.

A wealth of pain returned as I laid back in the bath. My mind wandered to the year MMIII. This time was no different from other moments I have chosen to ignore the past.

This time was different. This time I chose to give my past the energy it deserved. This time, I worked with myself to heal. Times in the past I wondered if the year MMI-II would have been different if my life had no input from Ricardo. It is the biggest kept secret between my parents and I. None of my siblings knew anything about it and I couldn't stop myself spiralling.

That being said, at this point my mother knew nothing about Ricardo. Her and my father were collectively disappointed and that hurt me the most.

Looking back, I question if it was a lack of self-love or family love which drove my desire to want to master the art of escapism.

***

'How did we miss this?' I heard my mother's voice break through my haze.

'Why did she not come to us?' She continued and I heard tears in her voice. 'I wish she came to us instead of having gone through this alone.'

I didn't know who it was she was speaking to as there was no reply, but the stillness caused me to hear a beep I recognised, the continuous kind heard when watching movies and someone was in the hospital.

Was I in the hospital?

I slowly opened my eyes to face reality. I was met with my fear, I was in the hospital, which only means I have failed. My hands automatically moved to my stomach and a sigh escaped. Regret washed over me. I failed at something which should have been easy. One job. Only one job.

'What did we do wrong?' My mum's voice broke more.

'We can only ask her that question.' I heard my father's voice laced with disappointment.

If only the Earth could do me a favour and pull me into Her core, I'd be happy. I have let my parents down and how to face them is not something I think I can do just yet. How was I going to explain why it was that I filled my system with ibuprofen, naproxen and amoxicillin. It would mean that I truly got myself into a predicament which only had two exits, and the one I chose led me here.

I opened my mouth to speak, yet it felt as though I swallowed the Sahara desert. I closed my mouth just to try again, but nothing. The desert was still present. I didn't want to clear my throat for my presence to be acknowledged just as yet but I needed for this desert's presence to be drowned; if only this drowning could be caused by the guilt which was washing over me.

I tightly closed my eyes in hope that the tears which now threatened to drench my face would be redirected to my throat. Wishful thinking. Clearing my throat, I instead hesitantly opened my eyes.

I saw their bodies as though they were floating to lift themselves to be above me. Drifting closer, my mind raced as though it were in Formula 1 against Lewis Hamilton. My body shifted uncomfortably, pathetically.

'Baby.' My father placed his hand on mine. His eyes were heavy. I saw the pain. I saw the way he would forever look at me. I saw the dredge for an explanation. I felt his love and warmth as he bent over to kiss my forehead.

My mother stood close but said nothing. Her eyes looked familiar to the blood I saw dripping from my arm as I laid in the bath. She cried. I saw the stain from her tears parting her makeup on both sides of her cheeks. I couldn't tell if she still loved me at that moment and I wouldn't be upset if she had lost love for me; I no longer loved myself.

She placed a glass with a straw in it to my mouth. 'Sip.'

'Ah, someone is awake.' A nurse smiled as she walked into my cubicle. 'How are you feeling?'

I lowered my eyes. How did I feel? Angry. Mortified. Remorseful. Displeased. Tired. Nothing to say happy. But what was I to tell her? Do I say one of these words to her. Do I tell her I'm okay? Do I tell her that I don't know. Am I meant to be in physical pain? What is it I am to say to her?

'Okay I guess.' My voice said.

'Okay is good.' She continued to smile. It was warm. Her presence managed to fill the room with the light which was missing from my parents.

'I'm just going to check your vitals Niyah.' She placed the pulse oximetry on my finger before placing the blood pressure cuff on my upper left arm. She took my readings from the machine before removing everything from my body.

'Everything looks fine.' She smiled as she placed the clipboard with my details on it at the front of my bed.

I know I needed to ask the question, but I felt a fire within me. I felt empty, but I needed the confirmation. I had to be told. I wrestled with myself. There was a war going on between my heart and brain. My spirit needed to know. That's the only way I could begin the conversation with my parents. Indirectly being honest with them by asking her.

I swallowed and took a deep breath as I watched her pulling the curtain slightly to leave.

'Nurse.' I said hoarsely.

'Yes.' She turned to me.

'What about the baby?' I looked directly at her avoiding the glares I know I'd be receiving from my parents.

Her smile faded and that's when I knew. I wouldn't be a teenage parent. I wouldn't miss my opportunity to go to university. I wouldn't be a drop-out.

One of the biggest mistakes for me to make, I made at the age of 18 and my immature and selfish mind at that point thought I did one of the best things for myself. I may not have managed to kill myself, a musical I would need to approach with care at a later stage, but I did manage to lose a child, my first child, in the process.

At the age of 18 in 2003, I had no idea that this loss of my child would come back to haunt me. I didn't realise that this would be a wound I would find difficult to heal. Back then, as I laid on that hospital bed and saw the light leave the nurse, I thought it was the biggest saving grace for me.

'You lost the baby Niyah.' She said to me.

Mum sobbed. Her sobs turned into chokes. Her chokes morphed into breathtaking crying. My baby didn't survive my suicide attempt and I was pleased, but my mother took it hard. My father held her as she buried herself in his chest.

I wished for a river to drown the water within my cells. To fill my lungs and empower my body. I had killed a piece of my mother. Her inability to punctuate her cries struck every part of me. Dad took her out of the cubicle leaving me alone with my thoughts.

A date for me to forget, my mind promised. Without my permission, instead it clung to it. Sunday 12th January 2003. The day I killed pieces of my parents. I stopped them from becoming grandparents. I stopped them from becoming sole carers of a fourth child. An unplanned child. Their grandchild.

I knew this was the date as my mother still had her church dress on, without the big hat and my father was still in his church suit, without his tie. They were both dishevelled because I didn't think to speak to them before trying to take my life. Instead, I overdosed, ran the bath, and with each thought, ran the razor along my wrist as the water changed from clear to pink. The blood wasn't enough to change it completely. Blood was not thicker than water. I proved it.

It didn't hurt then. What hurts is knowing that I inadvertently took their trust away from me. They didn't know I was no longer a virgin, let alone know I was pregnant. Something I hid from them for 2 months. It plagued me each day from finding out. So I chose to stay home that day. I said I wouldn't go to church because I was tired and needed the energy to do some revision later on that day.

As I laid in the bath today, I could see my body curled up in bed as I allowed the baby in my mind to become a monster. My baby. I turned my baby into a monster. The monster that was not under my bed, or in my wardrobe. My baby became the monster within me and I needed to do something to remove it. I couldn't allow it to be born, but I couldn't bring myself to punch it, so I researched ways in which I could kill it without going to the doctors again. That would have been another lie to tell, so I researched.

I searched the cupboards in the kitchen and found Charlene's amoxicillin along with the ibuprofens that were in the house in case of emergency. I cried as I allowed the bath to fill with water. I stole the razor from my dad's sheer kit. Ever so often he would use the razor to shave his beard, I knew it. I went for it. I needed it. My actions may have forced my parents to think they were incompetent, but what they didn't know was I felt compelled to prove to myself that I could have the power over whom I had intercourse with.

These guys who were nothing but meaningless to me were victims of my past and if I were able to apologise to them all separately, I would. I would go back in time and stop them from getting involved with me at that time. I would have searched their souls to see them as Kings instead of disposables.

Though my siblings, Charlene and Nick, knew I overdosed, neither were aware that I had also miscarried. This shame upon my parents, a residual effect of my trauma faced as a child, was kept between us. Us three, a trinity of misfortune. The trinity of my sin.

In hindsight, that was more detrimental than me withholding the truth from them. We hid the truth from the rest of the family which meant that Ricardo was never able to get the help he truly deserved. This meant we were the gatekeepers of the truth which could have saved Avery, his niece.

Amends need to be made with my past and I can't help but think I too am responsible for the actions Ricardo took to continue with his devious ways. He was caught fondling her one afternoon, I was told. Her parents left her with dear uncle Ricardo though she protested. They wanted to have their regular date night but had to return home abruptly. Why this was the case, no-one knows, but my mother told me that once they got home, they saw him with his hand in her knickers. That's when they truly began listening to Avery. She had been telling her parents that her uncle Ricardo touched her, but they blamed her vivid imagination because he denied everything.

Avery was brave. She did what I found impossible to

do as a child for I thought I wouldn't be believed. She wasn't believed but it had not deterred her to continue her protests against seeing him.

I have suggested that they see a family counsellor or a counsellor solely for Avery to discuss the trauma she had faced. They decided against my suggestion as pride stopped them from seeking to take this to anyone. Pride stopped them from turning Ricardo in to the police.

Pride continues to kill the flame within the souls of those who have been sexually assaulted as children. Pride continues to be the monster who looms above those who wish to be able to speak and heal from their trauma.

It will take time for Avery to heal if David and his wife will not come to terms with the impact this will have on Avery's adulthood if she is unable to speak with a professional about this. Had this trinity between my parents and I not been formed, I would have been able to take this further with them and speak to Avery myself. Allow her to know she is not the only one to have faced the wrath of her uncle.

It has now been three years since she has had to walk with the burden of the pain she faced. She too was in a trinity with her parents and I would love to help her to stop her from making the mistakes I did or going the other way feeling as though she was worthless and hiding her body as the shame would have stolen her self-love. No thirteen year old should have to walk with her uncle's unhealthy actions as her burden.

Well Orion, I'm going to take some time to meditate and do my yoga. I am still healing.

With purpose, I'm signing that my crown is cherished.

Niyah Adenike Thomas.

Aug. 2019

Dear Orion,

Love is a difficult tree to climb when you do not understand where to place your hands or feet. Whenever you feel you've found out how to move onwards and upwards, something comes back to haunt you and pushes you down. Features of an individual that causes you to love them are the same features that bring pain. That feature has been my love and pain, hands. What should be loving is also a death trap. Where I had not healed from my past, I fell into traps which took more of my love away. It killed my ability to find the strength within to love myself.

Hands have always been an interesting feature on a human's body to me. They hold so many hidden stories our eyes at times miss. No matter how ageless some faces may seem, our hands do not fail to hide the years that have passed us by.

Others speak about eyes being the windows to one's soul. Whilst psychologists say a more symmetrical face is more attractive. They've even said that individuals with symmetrical, aesthetically pleasing faces tend to get lighter sentences in the court of law. As for me, I've always been drawn to looking at hands. There's something about them which grabs my attention and at times I do feel like a creep. I find myself on trains staring at the hands of strangers as though they are portals to a dimension I'm hoping to explore.

One of my past lovers had hands that spoke differently to me, hands that spoke differently to me, I always felt trapped whenever he touched me. They were enchanted. However, for some time, for some reason, I missed them. I missed the callous feel of the love he showed.

What's worse, though unreal, it was the best yet.

I missed that though they read my body well, they knew what pages to disregard enough yet still have me clinging on for an ending better than the beginning. His hands were the perfect cliffhangers.

Now each time I seem to catch sight of new hands, I create stories in my mind about them. Stories of hope. These new hands have never left visitors fearing for their lives. They are instead sensitive. Eradicating pain and exercising patience.

Today was that kind of day. The one which made me excited and, as IndiaArie said, Ready for Love. At the same time, I was drenched with anxiety. My heart jumped through hoops, I felt as though the palpitations were my soundtrack for an hour. I know it didn't last that long, but the come and go seemed to have gone on for that long.

Is there something auspicious about my seeing 11:11 as I've just briefly looked up at the TV? It was the time on a digital clock in a movie. Not sure what exactly was happening in that precise moment, just noticed the time.

Okay, where was I? Today. Hands.

On my way to the office, I saw a gentleman with very familiar hands. I was lost in a book and as I've just done, looked up without reason, and noticed his hands. Taken aback, I jumped slightly. No warning, my heart raced and that was the beginning of the palpitations.

My mind was still fixated on the familiarity of his hands, I couldn't seem to take my eyes away from them. I felt my body fold in on itself and this was my breaking point.

With my palpitations looped, I entered into flashbacks.

Memories I have tried to suppress all came flooding in. The most haunting were memories of him. When we first met, he had an air of serenity about him. He felt as though he knew how to deliver love. The more we spoke, the more I learnt that he was a storm, what he presents in public, was the eye. In private, his surface winds were exceptionally strong.

Our relationship lasted for two years; most of my time was spent battling his destruction.

* * *

'You know you aren't special right?' He snarled as his left hand held my hands above my head. His right held my head firmly in place so I couldn't look anywhere but his eyes.

'Black women always think they own the Earth' he continued. His hands tightened around my body. He reminded me of a python forcing me to remain still, no sudden movements to protect myself from him devouring me.

I hate snakes. There and then, I hated him.

'Every time you lot get an inch of love you get excited and try get more out of men. You don't deserve something you don't even know how to give.' I felt my eyes well up. I could see the brokenness in him. I wanted to forgive him, but his hands kept squeezing. They held me in position. I became his artwork, moulded in place for him to exert his authority.

As I read his eyes, I remembered how his hands once read my soul with tenderness, as though it was written in braille.

* * *

Before the control became normal, he would jokingly say things that would attack my past. It should have been a warning sign. Though uncomfortable, I laughed along as I desperately wanted to prove to the 7 year old in me that she was deserving of love. Someone out there would love that she was given a name with such power and authority.

The years of hardship I endured would graze across my skin. My soul would cave in on itself as his hands searched for it. I couldn't hear my intuition clearly so I was stuck. His veins, hued purple, popped beneath his flesh. His knuckles on high alert waiting for my wrong move. All nails cut low, except that of his pinky; 'it's none of your business' he'd tell me.

His face was soft. A neat, well-kept beard clung to his caramel skin. Lips ready for a warm embrace. A nose wanting to be nuzzled into the nape of a neck. And eyes with pain beneath their surface, yearned what his hands suffocated.

On his own in public, I've watched as he picked at his nail bed, wringing hands together, he'd make eye contact with no-one. He looked nervous, shy even. At home, he morphed into an unrecognisable being.

I loved him all the same. At least that's what he told me.

His control was easy.

I had a strained relationship with my family and very few friends whom I rarely saw. This meant I was more malleable. Outsiders were unaware of our tumultuous relationship. I was unsavable.

Lust bit hard on shoulder blades
Overtly exerting itself
Villainising an untainted karma
Instructing monstrosities upon peaceful souls
Nearing end times
Becoming gimmicks of what should be perfect.

Lust trapped his soul in hell's pit
Me, the epitome of his escape
My body, his land to be marked
His hands, the cuffs I was unable to be free from.

Lust made me stay.
You ask why I stayed,
But you didn't ask about my mind.

You didn't ask about the strength taken from
me.
You didn't ask if I was able to rip lust from love.
You do not understand how similar he was to
the Earth.
I examined his outer layer,
It resembled the Earth
The Earth too looks beautiful from outer space.

Unconditional offers of
Never ending romance stones.
Longing for a yes,
Orienting a slight pang of pain.
Verifying what I've always known
Instead the pleads and painting
Notoriously kept me in this
Game of his, controlling none other than me.

Well Orion, it's getting late, so, here we are once again.

With purpose, I'm signing that my crown is cherished.

Niyah Adenike Thomas.

Dear Orion,

Ayomide has been a Godsend. She truly helped me to come into myself and out of my head. Over the course of our friendship, I have grown as a woman and a lover of myself.

The thing about Ayomide is that she is confident. She was brought up in a space where she was encouraged to not doubt her ability. I have been to her house when we were in Sixth Form and can remember her mother telling us that we should allow no-one to shake our self-confidence.

There was one occasion which truly got to me. I was dating a white guy, Callum, when we were in our second year of Sixth Form. He treated me like a queen. Never said a word to belittle me. Always held my hand whenever in public. Checked in on me every day and that fateful day came when I believed my heart was similar to a vase.

We planned to go to the cinema with Ayomide and her then boyfriend, one of his friends and his girlfriend. All was going well until we met up. His friend, not from our Sixth Form, commented on my appearance and the world suddenly stopped.

Ayomide wasn't there at the time, which may have been for the best. But my boyfriend was there. Callum was there but it felt as though he had been swapped with someone I didn't know.

I was horrified. My mind was blank. Callum and I were together for at least three months and I have never felt this much anger towards him. I was always so caught up in the bliss, I could not find fault to be angry at him.

Not until that moment. Not until he stood by and allowed his friend to disrespect me. Words had not cut so

deeply into my organs since Jah told me he hated me.
"She's actually pretty for a black girl, Callum."My eyes
widened.
"You did well." He continued.
My heart galloped. My breath quivered. I was dumb-
founded having heard the words escape his mouth.
'For a black girl?' I questioned.
'Yeah. It's not like you're white.' His brazen mouth con-
tinued.
Callum shrugged when I looked at him. His friend
laughed at my dismay. 'Why are you so shocked?'
I don't know what came over me. What I do know is
my fist connected with his jaw. No retaliation from him. I
think he was frozen from shock. Storming past him, I saw
Ayomide running towards me.
'Niyah what happened?'
I took slow deep breaths while staring ahead of me.
My feet hadn't stopped. I felt Ayomide by my side. One
hand on my lower arm, the other wrapped around my
waist, her head resting on my shoulder.
'She's actually pretty for a black girl' I mumbled. 'The
audacity.'
My fists clenched.
'For a black girl' I continued.
Having lost track of everything around, I hadn't noticed when we arrived at my house. We sat in the living
room. All walls bar one was painted white, a feature wall,
painted yellow with black floral silhouettes. Why yellow
of all the colours could have been chosen, I still do not
understand. My parents were with us. Dad in the arm-
chair by the window, Mum to my right, myself with Ayomide still on my left on the three seater by the feature
wall.
The silence stung. The repeated words in my head
didn't hush themselves. They only got louder.

I can feel my heart beating as loudly now as it did then.

'Who the hell does he think he is though?' My words cut through the belly of silence.

'Talking 'bout I'm actually pretty for a black girl.' I continued. 'I swear Callum is a wasteman! The two of them!'

'Callum said that?' My mum asked.

'Nah'. I gritted my teeth. 'His dumb friend that came cinema, but Callum just stood there and said nothing.'

Ayomide's hand gripped my arm. I turned to her 'that's why I rocked his jaw.'

'Should have told me so I could have done the same to Callum.' She chuckled and released her grip.

'Violence solves nothing.' My dad's voice, soft but stern, caused us to turn to him.

A sigh escaped.

'I didn't know what else to do.'

'Walk away.' He replied.

'*That* solves nothing and would leave them laughing.'

'You could be reported for assault. They would still laugh.'

'Well at least now he will know to think before he speaks.'

'Niyah, it doesn't justify your actions, no matter how you put it.' His voice with more pain than anger ripped through my belly.

'Your father is right Niyah.' Mum added. 'You know better. You have been taught better.'

I knew what they were saying was right but part of me knew walking away would have played on my mind a lot more.

In hindsight, I felt the violence should have been directed at Callum. Only to an extent. Let him feel how I felt. But that moment went. Well, that's a very sad joke. In honesty, today's version of that 17 year-old would have politely educated Callum and his friend.

I wasn't able to do so then. I still felt ugly *for a black girl.* Having a boyfriend willing to tell you how beautiful you are is only a plaster used to temporarily hide that scar.

My ideology of beauty was skin deep. Personality was a kite which soared above. This set me back. A lot. It bothered me then and in today's world, I'm trying my hardest to feed into my beauty.

It has always been difficult to feel beautiful as a black girl in a white society. Advertisements had always shown slender white girls as the definition of beauty. Only in recent times have they diversified their marketing strategies. And hello Rihanna. She has come through with the makeup for all shades of black. Who said black celebrities don't look out for their fellow people? Baby girl did that!

It's all come a long way with advertisements and products made for blacks. We are now seeing a surge of black made items for blacks and I am in love with it. Moving into a very Afrocentric world and it is one of the most beautiful things yet.

Had things been this lovely when I was younger, I think it would have taught Callum's friend something about black beauty. Not the horse, but the beauty of black people.

Today I imagine I know better
My beauty is the anchor from within
Where I fail to communicate love with others
I communicate with myself first
I stare into my brown eyes to understand
How best to spot lies.

I carry my heart in my hands
Exposing her to a world of pain
Embracing joy and happiness

She has to be renewed despite measures
To keep her trapped.

It's important to identify
The hours within the moments
We ought to show ourselves reality
I've learnt the hard way
Grace has been granted
I have been given chances
Now I will not self-sabotage
I come first.

It's now time Orion. Time for me to say goodnight.

With purpose, I'm signing that my crown is cherished.

Niyah Adenike Thomas.

Dear Orion,

My past has contributed to this muddied idea I have of what love should be.

Though my grandparents invested so much time in reminding me of how special I am, I lost that feeling of royalty they tried to tell me I had. I couldn't understand what my purpose was and how to live up to the idea that my crown is cherished. Having been told by my own blood that no-one likes me and another blood relation exploiting my body for his gratification, I didn't understand how to love myself. If those closely related to me based on our DNA chose to be so harmful to me, how could I love myself?

It made little sense as to why my boyfriend stood back and either said nothing as I was being belittled, or chose to physically abuse me.

My attitude towards men was not shaped by what I saw from my mother towards my father, or from her to other men who were either her friends or acquaintances.

Something in me feels as though my perception of these men and the way I treat them is related to the way I feel and have felt about myself. I have on many occasions questioned whether love stems from the well within, or the fountain of family lessons?

As foreign as it feels, love is a complexity within family systems but also on an intrapersonal level. Some consider it to be innate, something we were born to do. They say a child is taught to hate, but does this not also mean that a child is also taught how to love? Both are opposing factors. How can you know one without being intro duced to the other? Additionally, if love is innate, does that not also mean that hate is also an innate emotion? A very interesting view around love is that it comes from one's consciousness, where external factors have an effect as they are the variants that cause us to determine how we feel about and towards someone or something.

Love differs amongst individuals. Whether this is to do with the beliefs their parents or carers taught them, experiences they have faced, or research they may have done, it still shows that love is not as simple as classifying animals or extracting DNA to be compared. The commonality between them all is love is a result of that which occurs in the external world. To them, that is the cause which shifts the flow of their energy. I think we can, therefore, agree that it isn't tangible. The similarities and dissimilarities show how much it varies from person to person.

To me, love is a wish-wash painting not to be understood all in one breath taken. Love is like a Microsoft Package, upgraded often enough when loopholes are found in the current version to be able to mend and make it better. This package also removes that which isn't relevant for individuals, not that one person is more important than another, but, it may, at that time be all too overwhelming for them.

I was fortunate to be raised in a house which allowed me to witness a grounded love between my parents. My siblings too, but it seems we are from two different worlds when I compare the way we all treat love. I understand individual differences and how each person's mindset choreographs their actions in ways unspeakable. However, what I am growing to know is how it is that siblings, all treated with the same love, have responded differently to how they choose to love.

Ever since the 31st of July, I have been spending more

time thinking about my past trying to work through it. I should see a therapist, but am finding it so difficult to bring myself to doing so. It's hypocritical that I say my younger cousin should see a therapist, yet I won't. I know my trauma is so deeply etched, it would take a lot of breaking down before I was to be able to be rebuilt. She is younger and easier to be rescued than I am. Had I been working as a counsellor, I would have had a counsellor for myself. However, my job is a family coach, my background is in social work. I am yet to return to work but am taking it a day at a time. I took a week off work as suggested by my manager who noticed upon my return to work on Thursday that I was still overwhelmed. I have been using the time to unpick my problems a day at a time. Meditation and yoga have proven to be sufficient along with spending time reading the Bible and praying.

During my search on the internet of what the Bible says about love, I came across a suggestion found in Proverbs 10 verse 12, 'Hatred stirs up strife, but love covers all offenses'. It wasn't particularly clear to me; should I still love Ricardo though he molested me? Was it because Ricardo hated me why he molested me? I wish I had a pastor or priest whom I could call and discuss this with. I stopped going to church when I moved out of my parents' house. Church felt too much like a punishment for the reminder I hated to have about Sunday 12th of January in 2003.

To be honest, reading through Proverbs 10 didn't make me feel much better about my circumstances. It heightened so much more of a feeling of dread within myself. I won't know if it is a good or bad thing just yet, but I do know it's been a difficult day for me. Verse 6 for instance says that those who are righteous will have blessings but it is violence which is concealed by the mouth of the wicked. I wouldn't particularly class myself as a wicked person, however I know I am not righteous. This idea of the righteous being blessed and the wicked technically being cursed runs through and my mind enjoys the playing field it has been allowed to wander into.

I thought, as with textbooks, the answer would have been within the rest of the passage. Nothing before or after verse 12 gave me the answer I was after.

I continued with my search on the internet. I needed something to make sense to me. I needed something to give me the hope and guidance I needed.

To move forward, one needs to take a step backwards, and my backwards was to slip into the world of my parents. Find the relationship they have with God, find one for myself. I'm not sure it's possible to get that within a day, but I needed answers. Though the possibility may be slim, I began to see clearer. There were other scriptures about love that helped me to piece together the definition of the love Christians know and speak well of. Take First Peter 4 verse 8 *'above all, keep loving one another earnestly, since love covers a multitude of sins'* and John chapter 13 verses 34 – 35 *'a new commandment I give to you, that you love one another: just as I have loved you, you also are to love one another. By this all people will know that you are my disciples, if you have love for one another'.* I'm not claiming that I am a disciple and maybe I won't be, but I can say I get it. It makes sense now! If I love Ricardo, it would go hand in hand with what I understand about forgiveness. By forgiving and loving him, it means I will not think ill things against him.

I've never not loved Ricardo. He is family and I remember my parents saying that no matter what, particularly my mother as that was her nephew, I was to still love him. How was I to love someone who infected me with their sickness? The invisible form, the mental type. The one no-one spoke of because we were black and that was for the other kind of people. The white people. Ricardo was sick. He had an obsessive trait which started within his mind. He passed this onto me when he molested me on countless occasions. I became depressive and suicidal after becoming addicted to sex to run away from my childhood horror show.

I struggled with depression for years, this is why I had a breakdown. I had depression at the age of 18, this is why I attempted suicide.

I was not allowed to speak of it.

Instead, we would pray the demons away which plagued my mind. Yet, I was not schizophrenic. I had no hallucinations, delusions or disorganized thinking. Yet, I was treated as though I was hearing voices in my head. I needed to hear the voice of God; I think I am hearing it now telling me to love and forgive in order to move forward.

I was and am still dealing with my depression. One day at a time. I have over the years found ways to help myself without going to the doctor's office. I have self-medicated with alcohol, drinking each night after work. When that stopped working, I found a guy whom I could have sex with, someone I would never need to see again, a one-night stand.

Come to think about it, I now do not know why I was so shocked when Kyron had offered to be my booty call. I have had one-night stands before he came along. I was never the virtuous woman I told myself I wanted to be. God already knows my heart, it's just that you didn't know who I was and I felt if I told you that, it would make me feel better about myself.

There is so much hiding and lying I can do before my soul catches on. How will I be able to heal if I am not open with you? If I cannot be open with you, how will I be able to see a therapist? How will I tell them the truth? How will my money be spent wisely for self-development?

Well Orion, that's it from me today. You know what

came to mind, Well Orion, that's it from me today. You know what came to mind, Bugs Bunny when he says 'that's all folks' at the end of Looney Tunes. It was Looney Tunes right? Well, I'll be going, we won't spend long delving into whether that was Looney Tunes or not. I've got a missed call and think I'll return it.

With purpose, I'm signing that my crown is cherished.

Niyah Adenike Thomas.

Confession #2:

I have never had girlfriends to enjoy nights with.
We wired and wounded
Wind up weaving fun into our lives
We exchange no tears
Instead, spin the arrow for shots
Shooting alcohol into our veins
Preparing for a night of highs
A night where no mishap can
Infiltrate our thoughts.

<u>Sunday 4th August 2019</u>
<u>Time: 17:17</u>

Dear Orion,

The world felt wrong today. My head still kills and my body is too heavy for me to lug around. I think I do have it in me to tell you about my adventures last night.
I feel better. Somewhat.
My decreased alcohol intake has meant that I am now unable to hold my liquor as I did once upon a time. Being at my friend Deja's house last night involved a lot of drinking and dancing then drinking again. She didn't know the things that have been bothering me. What she did know was that I've been off work and won't be back until next Monday, so she invited me to her house.
She invited me, having finally gotten a hold of me. We spoke for two hours, twelve minutes, and twenty-two seconds, 2:12:22, after I had written to you yesterday. Isn't it funny that yesterday was the first day I told you the time and I then took notice of the time once I got off the phone to Deja? I know it's something she's into, so I'll talk to her tomorrow when my brain can handle that communication.
Back to me telling you about last night. The music was loud. Each bass line pulsed through my core. With each vibration, my body swayed. I drank. We drank. The alcohol loosened our muscles and slowly the lyrics became one with us. The rhythm, our dance partners. We sang with Whitney saying how much we wanted to dance with somebody who we could feel the heat with. Our bodies moved simultaneously with the freedom which pumped through Deja's speakers.
As heavy as my body is at this moment, I have no regrets. I have never felt so weightless before. I know it isn't

the alcohol which took over. My mind was clear. I had no thought of any burdens which have been haunting me. I was in a safe space with women who were not judgemental of me or my past. These women helped me to see I was not alone.

All hard working. All successful in what we do. But we all had a darkness within which tried to consume us. Tried to consume them. I was failing the battle to remain whole during my turmoil. And the amazing thing about last night, none of them made me feel worse than I was feeling at the time.

They consoled me. Lifted my spirit. Cathy told me about an app which would help me to focus and maintain my strength within. Nicola told me about books I could read to help with my growth. Deja topped up my glass when it ran low. Her job was already done by spending over two hours with me on the phone. All in all, these ladies filled me with a warmth I've only ever received from Ayomide.

Interesting that in that moment I would feel such familiarity or love. The return of Philia. The only person I have had this love for over the years has been Ayomide, and now, I had other women with whom I can share it. Philia is an affectionate kind of love which is felt for friends.

Orion, my head hurts but everything is now coming together. The names. Their meanings. My friends. My view on love. How to navigate in this horror show I am living. If I don't do this now, it's going to bother me for the rest of the day and I swear, my head hurts way too much for me to go through this for the rest of the day. I've got to find the meaning of the other girls' names.

I've always been big on the meaning of names, especially of those who come into my life, no matter how short a period they are in my life. My grandparents didn't realise what they were doing when they kept reminding me of the definition of my name. They planted within me this curiosity to see how a person's name links with their personalities. As Deja is into numerology, I am into names and their definitions. I can't yet seem to find a word which defines it, but that's the case.

Ayomide's name means joy has arrived. I remember the day I asked what her name meant. It was at the end of sixth form, we planned to spend the day in Greenwich. We went to the cinema and spent the rest of the time in the park. I can't remember what we watched but the time we spent in the park remains within my memory.

We were anxious about our A-Level results. We knew we did all that we could. Revised every day. Practically lived in the library. We were still anxious, and, as anxious as I felt, it wasn't as bad within her presence as it was when I was at home.

***

'Ayo, what does your name mean?' I looked up from the ice lolly I had broken in half.

'Woman why?' Her eyebrows furrowed.

'I'm curious and have never asked you.'

'Who knows the meaning of their names?'

'I do.'

'So, what does it mean then?'

'Niyah means purpose and Adenike means cherished crown. Now stop evading my question and give me an answer.'

'Wasn't evading. Just –'

She paused, holding her face towards the sun, eyes closed, a lax smile walked across her face. I saw peace cover her. She looked weightless; as light as a feather.

'Just what?' I asked.

'I have never believed that names held power over anyone, so dismissed it.'

'But they do.' I replied. 'My grandparents always said they do. They hammered that into my head when I was growing up.'

'And what if nothing truly aligns with the definition of your name?'

'Nothing aligns with what my name means but I still continue.'

There was something about the ice lolly I had in my hand. I really wanted a suck suck or even a bag juice. For some reason they tasted better than these. A suck suck is made by mixing drinks, putting them into a clear plastic bag, tying and freezing them. Freeze-pop in a bag. Bag juice is the same but sealed differently and I think those are made in factories. Thoughts of these made me nostalgic for a home which was my frequent holiday destination.

'My name means my joy has arrived.'

'That's a beautiful meaning!' I almost leapt into the air.

'Is my joy arriving though Niy?' She looked me in the eyes. 'My dad's got cancer. My grandmother just passed away. Mum's having difficulties at work because she is black. No happiness is coming Niyah.'

'I didn't know things were so difficult for you Ayo.' My lips folded in on themselves.

'Why didn't you say something?'

'Because I didn't want to burden you with my worries.'

'You wouldn't have been a burden though.' I gave her my as-a-matter-of-fact look. 'And, you bring joy with you wherever you go. I think that's what your name means.'

'So I bring joy to others and it gets taken from me?'

'It's not taken from you. You see the good in everyone else's mishaps. You have helped me enough times to get over my problems. You do the same for others. You help us to see the good in things, to feel better.'

I took another bite of my lolly.

'I'm not and will never say that baba having cancer orthat Gogo passing on or ìyá being mistreated at work is a good thing, but I'm saying that you are joy. You can be the joy for your parents during this time. You can bring joy to your family. And think about it, how many times has ìyá said you've brought joy to her life?'

'I swear I can't stand you.' She said as tears rolled down her cheeks. 'You just love to make sense don't you?'

'Why not?' We both laughed.

***

Deja's name is interesting. She makes me feel nostalgic and at times I can't figure out what it is she reminds me of or who or what time. She just has an air of familiarity which never fails to bring me peace. The way she makes me feel always reminds me of the meaning of her name. Sometimes it makes me afraid as I feel I will begin to dig up unresolved issues, but that's never been the case. It's the warmth which she reminds me of.

Now for the other two girls. I've only just met them last night so the internet and I are about to have a little relationship as I search their names.

Cathy's name is from the names Catherine, Katharina, Caitlin and Aikaterina. Online it says that these names are from four backgrounds; French, Greek, Irish and Latin, all meaning the same thing, pure. Based on her energy last night, before the flow of the alcohol, she didn't seem like the person who would hide anything.

As for Nicola, her name is a derivative of the Latin, Greek and English names, Nikolaos and Nicholas both meaning victory of the people. Whether she has ever been aware of the meaning of her name I have no clue, but she has presented herself as someone who doesn't compete with others and is interested in seeing everyone win.

I couldn't have had a better night than last night and

to have met beautiful souls with such wonderful names gives me hope for a better tomorrow. Their names and personalities can only mean that things are going to work for my greater good; these women whom I'd love to spend time with again, are definitely my spirit guides.

Okay, I'm going to try to either do some yoga or curl up in my bed now. My head still hurts. I don't think I'll be drinking like that again.

Take care Orion.

Until next time.

With purpose, I'm signing that my crown is cherished.

Niyah Adenike Thomas.

Dear Orion,

I slept like a baby last night. I didn't really feel like cooking, so did the whole UberEats thing before bed; fried plantain, oxtail, rice & peas, coleslaw, and super-malt. I was in food heaven. I had never eaten from that restaurant before, but I have heard others talk about it, though honestly, everyone's idea of a nice Jamaican meal is not the same. I think I have come to conclude that some people have never had an A-class home cooked Jamaican dish.

That meal last night teleported me. Took me back to my childhood where we once had a family reunion in Jamaica. This was for my dad's side of the family. I was 10 years old and had never met many of my cousins before. Just like my mother's family, the majority of dad's family lived abroad. At this time, technology wasn't the biggest thing and communication I remember was either phone calls or letters. Christmas letters were the best. An aunt or uncle would send money for my siblings and I and there were the photos of other family members, you were able to see how much we were all growing up.

The day I remembered, we were on the beach, the music drowned out the sound of happiness, as the joy which shone from everyone's radiant body was brighter than the sunshine. IsAunty Joy in her apron had a cigarette in her mouth and a red stripe beer in her right hand, dancing without a care in the world. She looked as though she was in a meditative state. Her children ran up to her, but lost in her trance they were unable to get their mother's attention.

Dad came to me with a plate. My first family reunion.

First time meeting my overseas family. My first time eating Aunty Joy's food.

Not sure what to expect, I timidly lifted the fork to my mouth. Looking over at my aunt, I placed the fork in my mouth and I was certain I could taste the love she cooked with. Similar to last night's meal. I pictured the chef to have been rocking meditatively in love as they cooked.

To feel such love slip down your throat as you eat is the best feeling one could ever receive. I do not cook when I'm in a funk, I'm quite certain I get stomach aches when I do.

That meal left me in a deep state of thought though.

How is it that you can love someone you have never seen? Someone whom you may never meet. How do you cook so lovingly for them? Is love blind? How is it that it can be sent through meals? They say the way to a man's heart is through his stomach, does that make me a man because I can feel the love in meals? Do men determine how much they love a woman based on how much love he tastes from her meals? What if a woman cannot cook?

Marcel was like that. He is a friend I met in university. Our friendship was built solely on the basis that neither of us wanted relationships, but were happy to spend every waking second together. Marcel was my faithful customer who would never allow me to serve him. He told me on many occasions that it is the King who is to wait on the Queen, serve her as and when she desires. He did cook for me on a number of occasions, but cooking was mainly my thing, so long as he could serve me.

According to Ayomide, we were the perfect couple. Marcel and I, we were the perfect friends. He taught me a lot about love and its importance. The man, he would tell me, is to serve, support, and uplift the Queen. Though society and the Bible says that he is to be the breadwinner, that doesn't mean that the woman should fear going for a job which would pay her more than her spouse. No matter what she earns, it shouldn't stop him from supporting her. Her money, he emphasised, was hers. The money the man earns belongs to both. Lessons I think are of importance in today's day and age.

It was easy for me to agree with him as he lived by what he spoke. Though we were friends, when we went out, I was never allowed to use my money to buy anything. I was able to buy gifts for him for his birthday and Christmas, that was no problem. However, if we went to a restaurant, coffee shop, or even the cinema together, he paid. In the beginning we had little arguments about who would pay because I was always willing to pay my own way. I never wanted to feel dependent on him for anything. What he showed me was that I wasn't dependent as I still had my financial freedom.

The most difficult thing to learn and appreciate however was that no man owes that to me.

Marcel taught me my worth. He taught me that there is a difference between knowing my worth and expecting to be treated as the Queen I am. How a man treats me is based on his understanding of his own worth as well as being able to not be intimidated by my fire within. The fire I have is my self-worth. How brightly this fire burns is dependent on my ability to trust myself and be confident enough to stand by my worth. No-one needs to stand around and treat me how I expect to be treated, but they need to know and understand that I will not change the way I am to feed their ego. Because of Marcel, I believed love wasn't blind, but love was a gift to be shared.

This gift, shared through food, music, poetry, art, attitudes, is done from a place where an individual is able to see themselves in others. For one to see themselves as deserving of love, they are able to choose to give that love away. This complexity was beginning to make sense to me. The philosophy of it all was slowly being revealed to me as a simple solution.

The solution was to tend to the flame within me so that it would not consume or mislead me. Allow the flame to light a path which needs to be lit and not use it as a weapon. This fire needs to be worked on by cultivating a safe space for my present by revisiting the past one thread at a time.

It does get difficult though. Last week was proof of that.

I am grateful for my meal last night. The love the chef added to it was the perfect reminder I needed to lead me to meditate. Through meditation, I remembered my lessons from Marcel. I think I might have summoned him because he called me this morning, an hour before coming to you. The best call I could have ever received. This guy was my Santa Claus. He knew I wasn't sleeping and knew I needed to talk. He couldn't have called me at a better time than then.

Time check 11:00.

My body started to get so stiff, I had to step back and stretch. I forgot I hadn't done my yoga before Marcel rang, but my body didn't.

Though he was the same and sounded so good on the other end of the phone, something was different. His voice was trying to hide the truth which his heart wanted to share. He sounded troubled, but if he is still the same, he would not want me to know what it was. I had never seen him cry, nor has he ever spoken about crying. His views about men crying was all too familiar.

He was brought up on the foundation that boys should not cry. I have seen him at breaking point, remembering when his father passed away; I saw in his eyes he wanted to cry, but the comments of elders pulled his tears that they would not roll down his cheeks.

Marcel, as much as he believed in the love which should be extended, he failed to share it with himself. It's as though all he taught me was insignificant in relation to him. He was willing to express to me that I needed to grow into my worth and let my confidence guide me, but he couldn't do the same for himself.

He was a juxtaposition. Perfect contradiction.

This man knew how to make a woman feel like she was more than the gravity which kept her on the ground but failed to see he too was worthy. Worthy enough to walk into a room, stand firm in his truth and be unshakeable.

As much as he once encouraged me to open up and feel free enough to be honest with him, it wasn't reciprocal. He told me why he couldn't be open with me saying 'a Queen should never be burdened with the worries of a King'.

I know I wasn't obligated to hear his worries as it wasn't something he owed me. However, this he owed himself. I wasn't able to put into words then what I can now, but he was entitled to be free within himself, to be able to trust enough and allow someone to share love with him in his vulnerable state.

This was a common case of being told boys should not cry and men should be strong. What was always missed from the agenda was that crying was not the definition of being weak and strength would never be lost when lips parted to share troubles.

If a man is unable to be vulnerable enough with his partner, can he truly love her? Without self-love, are we able to empower ourselves enough to remain as one with the woman who has shared her heart with him?

I saw Marcel as a man who deserved to be loved by a

strong woman. A strong Black Woman.

I can't see him with a woman of a different ethnicity because he has always dated Black Women, but it doesn't mean he will not date outside the race. All he needs to do is allow himself to be vulnerable enough with the right woman so his heart feels comfortable to open.

Remember when I said black men had it harder than black women? This is one of the reasons. It's okay for me to want the best for my friend when it comes to relationships, but to know that there are so many of us as women who belittle our Black Men, it is no surprise when they fail to bare their souls with us.

We have skipped communication and expect that they should be emotionless yet very understanding.

One too many times I have witnessed black women placing blame on their male counterpart; 'he just don't get it' I would hear her saying to her friends, followed by 'leave him. If he don't want to talk to you and he won't listen to you, just leave him.' Her friends, world's best advisors would tell her to leave her other half. Rarely do I hear the suggestion that she should try to speak with him.

I have met with families separately, the wife or mother, followed by the husband or father, no children at these sessions, and the streams of consciousness seems to be universal. These men, I have been told, do not step up to the plate often enough. Yet, speaking to the men separately, it's a different story. They disclose more to me than they had ever done to their other half.

When I've dug deeper, asked about their families and how their parents have communicated, it solidifies my theory that we project what we have learned onto our partners. For me, this is one reason I am scared of being in a serious relationship. We take on traits from our parents which manifests themselves in the way we relate to our partners as well as how we raise our children.

Like Marcel, many of our black men are led to believe they must shoulder the burdens of their black women, friends and lovers without being able to share the load. This is similar for our females, but these women are more likely to speak their minds. If not to their other half, they have their girlfriends to share with. Our men do suffer more as they can't open up with their male friends. They are mocked and ridiculed because the majority tend to hold the belief that they should be silent about their emotions.

With the lack of speech, everything becomes bottled up. What these men fail to consider, once this bottle is full, if still being forced with more pressure, it will explode. They will explode. Then the terminology 'men are trash' escapes the woman's mouth and 'women are bitches' escapes his mouth.

How do we foster safe communities within ourselves to allow each other to be comfortable enough to release in a healthy manner? What can we do as women to help our men understand that their mental health is important enough to be maintained so they can be confident enough to share with us how they are feeling? How do we change loving them through their stomachs to loving them through their flaws as they do us?

And to return to Marcel, he and I got caught up during university. It was such a heavy conversation, but I told him everything that was on my mind about the way it all made me feel. I needed him to hear me and shared this with him:
Let me find your voice for you!

Because, right now,
This moment as I speak,
No one cares for you!
Let me

Find it in the belly of your pain
This heart wrenching burden you bare.
Let me
Dig through and find that
Golden tongue
Laced with hurt
Covered in a bile of lies.
Let me
Wipe it down
And not douse it in bleach
That it may not be sparkly and attractive
For its rawness is what is tantalising.

Let me
Charm the snake which sitteth upon thy tongue
That it too like the Phoenix will rise
Shedding its skin that the suppressed cries
from your gut
Will no longer linger beneath its belly
Which slithers around in your mouth
Taking pieces of you
Each time you open your eyes.

Let me find your voice for you.

And I take full ownership for you being a mute
So, I want to hold your murmurs in the palms of
my hands
To free you from your empirical mindset
Set in years of domesticated abuse because

You haven't even come to terms with
The funeral held for you when you entered this
world
And your mother's tears

Were a mixture of confusion.
She knew within herself that she would send you mixed signals,
Mainly signalling that you should always stifle your own tears
Though she shed many for you.
She knew she would tell you to keep your head up
That your vulnerability would not shine through
Because a glimpse of hurt was to only be shown by females
And you would not be taken seriously if you *ever* shed a tear.
Real men don't cry
And I am one of the reasons you are as fake as they get,
A counterfeit artefact wanting to be treated right
Yet my voice has only ever been extended for women.

Now I want to take it all back
Women are always being fought for
But never have we stopped to put you before us.
Yet they say behind every good man is a good woman
But we are no good for we force you to believe.
You are not allowed to cry
Nor are you allowed to show your emotion
Nor are you allowed to speak
For that all correlates with being weak
And that role was already taken by women
Not to be shared
But we are swift to say you need to learn to

communicate
When we already took your voice box
And tucked it away.

I'm sorry you've had to believe you are sound-
less
That your words should only relay
'I love yous'
Or
'You are beautiful'
Or
'What's for dinner?'
Or
Whatever else we expect to roll off your tongue
Which doesn't include
'Today was difficult for me'
Or
'It's all too much'
Or
'This is what's bugging me'

I'm sorry we've led you to believe
That you are of no importance more than
To insert below navel lines
Or to reach what's on the top shelf
Or to show off that manly body
Sliding your identity over our skins.
I'm sorry we've emasculated you.
We undoubtedly took all power from you
We've been fighting for our rights
Leaving you unsure
Not sure if you should stand up for you
Because, maybe, it would come across as
You being ungrateful because
You already get the better pay

And you are seen in society
And you have the big jobs
So, you can never go through anything we've
been through
How dare you open your mouth
To ask to be treated fairly
When we've stripped you of your humanness?
Let me be the one who takes on the role
To show you that I am no longer society,
I no longer believe a man should hide the way
he feels,
I no longer believe a man should not speak,
I no longer believe a man should be sexualised,
That us as ladies should drool over you.

As I spoke, I cried. I cried for him and the men in my family who were continuously told to stop the crying. I cried for the men I was yet to meet who struggled with crying. Marcel allowed my cries to fade as he held me in his arms. That was the moment he dubbed me as an advocate for males who had been silenced.

It was a moment. A name for the moment which stayed stuck in that space and time.

Well, I guess that's it from me today though Orion.

This is one of those things we must continue another day.

With purpose, I'm signing that my crown is cherished.

Niyah Adenike Thomas.

Dear Orion,

Boys should not hit girls, yet no-one tells girls they should not hit boys. Boys should not cry, that would make them as soft as a girl. Who on Earth thought that it was a good idea to be so sexist when speaking to children? Why are these ideas plus more taken into adulthood? Why has it taken so many years for individuals to come to an understanding that these are detrimental statements?

Marcel and I spoke about this today. We spoke for hours and he only recently left. Yes, he was here with me. He has taken annual leave which is why he called me yesterday and felt the need to see me today. I'm proud of him. Mr Big Shot. To see him was refreshing. His skin was so cool. His dark coffee complexion was smooth. Unlike the men I have been seeing around lately, his face was clean in comparison, neat beard and well-kept moustache. His build has changed though. No longer was he the scrawny boy I knew in university, something he said he hated about himself so spent hours in the gym, continuously. I did feel bad for pointing it out back then.

And that's how our conversation began.

'Why didn't you tell me you had a problem with calling you scrawny?'

'Because I never learnt how to let someone know that I didn't appreciate being put down.'

I looked into his eyes and saw a pang of pain behind his lids.

'I'm sorry Marcel.' I told him.

'Nothing to be sorry about Empress.' He smiled, but his smile didn't change the fact that I saw the pain he tried to hide. 'You and I were brought up to witness others unintentionally hurting others by taunting them right?'

'Yeah I guess so.'

'Now to add to that, mix the fact my emotions were always disregarded –' he paused.

'What do you mean?'

'Growing up. I couldn't cry about anything. If ever I were to cry, I would be told to stop the foolishness.'

'Sounds familiar.' Jah came to mind when he started crying and Papa told him that I should have been the one crying.

'Right. So, check it, to always be told that you need to stop crying translates to the idea that how way you feel is unimportant.'

'Therefore, it stopped you from telling anyone how their words affected you?' I asked.

'I always knew you were smart.' He mocked. I rolled my eyes with a smirk on my face.

...and the conversation continued. Another day for another lesson from this beautiful man.

'Our parents didn't need to think about what they were saying to us because they said what they were always hearing as they grew up. It became normal for them to speak down to us. Schools didn't really make it any better for boys. Boys would always be boys and we would be allowed to play fight with each other. Fights among us were normal. If one of us got mad and retaliated, we either fought or just left it there. When it came to girls, that was a different sort of conversation.' He took a sip of the water I gave to him when he arrived.

'I got in trouble back in Year 9 because I punched a girl. I tried to keep my cool but she kept pushing me and I got mad –' I raised my hand and stopped him mid sentence.

'You've got to restart this because I feel like I stepped

out of the room and caught the end of a conversation.' I raised my eyebrows as I spoke. My friend. The King who uplifted Queens had in his past life put his hand on a female.

He chuckled at my reaction. My hands were all over the place as I spoke, hitting every woah I threw and caught.

'You are something else Miss Thomas.' He shared the most beautiful smile with me in that instant.

'So' he started, rubbing his palms together as he replayed the moment in his mind. 'Me and this girl were together through Year 9, from the end of the summer holidays in Year 8 and I broke up with her because deep down I lost interest in her. She wasn't happy about it and kept coming up in my face and pushing me. She was shouting at me like crazy. She was vex. Pushed me while shouting 'why are you breaking up with me? I tried to ignore her as best as I could. But she prodded a little too hard and it wasn't until she started screaming that I didn't like her in the first place and was only with her to try to take her virginity, that I reached my breaking point with her.'

He pulled his left hand down his face.

'Niyah, I loved her. I actually loved her. I lost interest because I found out that she was sleeping with some of the Year 10s and didn't see why I should have stayed with someone who was cheating on me and giving up their body to everyone. But she wouldn't stop when I told her to. She hit me and hit me harder each time. I kept thinking, boys should not hit girls but she continued. I saw red in the end and punched her. Would have punched her again, but someone had jumped in to stop me. I don't remember anything else after that but sitting in my Head of Year's office.'

Tears began to trickle down his cheeks and I didn't know what to do. I froze. What do you do when a man begins to cry before you? Do you hug him? Do you let him cry into the air?

I sat there and watched him for a while but it didn't feel normal. To sit there and watch as he cried. I wouldn't have done that if Ayomide or Deja sat with me crying. I allowed my natural instincts to take over and sat next to him, holding him in my arms as he rested his head on me.

'I got excluded because I broke the rule. I punched a girl who was taunting me. A girl who was pushing and hitting me. I got excluded for a week and nothing happened to her. My Head of Year told me I knew better.' His body uncomfortably raised and fell in my arms as he cried.

'I got grounded for a month because I knew better. No-one cared to listen to me.'

We sat in the silence for what felt like hours. The only sounds which could be heard were the ticks of my clock and his soft sobs. It broke my heart to know this is what happens when our boys are repeatedly told they aren't to cry. These boys do not have any sense of what their voices sound like when they are hurt and they take this with them into adulthood. A burden they should not bear, but until we collectively teach them how to speak, this issue will persist and many more men will commit suicide. We've all heard the stats.

'Would you say anything's changed?'

'Yeah, I've not hit a female since.' He laughed. This was the same man who had been crying in my arms no more than 10 minutes ago.

'You are annoying!' I slapped him on his arm. 'Because you want to play like you don't understand, let me break it down for you. The way you view the dos and don'ts of the man. The dos and don'ts of the black man. The dos –'

'Yeah I have. My views have changed and I think I'm just learning how to get my actions to grow and match my views.'

I couldn't understand how such a beautifully crafted man could have struggles with his identity. I have always been interested in Marcel, not as someone I would date, but as a guide. My relationship with him was different from those I've had with other guys which I love.

'Any new relationships King?'

'Eww you want to talk about my love life.' He wrinkled his nose. Scrunched his face. Restricting his eyes from viewing the world well. His lips curled upwards.

'You look so cute when you do that.'

'There she goes ruining the moment.'

'Boy. Man. What moment?' Arms folded I looked at him.

'Nah Niy. I've been working on myself a lot you know. I've managed to work my way up and become a Band 7 Speech and Language Therapist. Next stop, Clinic Lead.'

If my walls could talk, they would have screamed at me for squealing. I had no idea I could shriek at such a high pitch, but it came out. I was so happy for Marcel. He has always been a hard worker and it made me feel blessed to know him.

'Love is complicated Niy. I want to believe in it, but it's something that's not easy to maintain.'

With that, Marcel told me about a relationship he was in for two years. An old friend of his with whom he fell in love with based on conversations they could have. What he failed to realise then, was this relationship he was in, is something his heart didn't want.

They were together because they were pressured by friends to pursue something further. Friends would say how well suited they were for each other, willing them to form something they could vicariously live through. They were to be the love story their friends wished for but were unable to find.

His story made me think about the values we place on

relationships and the reasons we seek them. Do we really understand what it is that we want from Eros? How much do we need to know about ourselves before we are able to delve into sharing it with others? Though there are lessons in every bond formed, if we were capable enough to venture into our hearts and understand what it wanted, maybe Eros would not be as difficult as it seemed to be.

I've not watched all the movies out there but I do know that I am yet to see the movie that shows a couple working on themselves individually before heading into a relationship. They tend to know what they want and have little idea of who they are when we see them, but their highs and lows are based on their lack. They operate based on their id, their instincts, and thus hidden memories manifest themselves in behaviours and how issues are handled.

I have one wish at this moment in time. At the start of my next relationship, I would like for us to discuss how we will not allow our instincts to take charge.

Enough of that from me. I'm going to enjoy dreaming about Marcel now. It's as good as everything gets for me.

With purpose, I'm signing that my crown is cherished.

Niyah Adenike Thomas.

Dear Orion,

With everything that came up yesterday in my conversation with Marcel, something has been playing on my mind. I feel this is the core of what makes us who we are and guides us in forming connections with others.

Identity.

I said it yesterday, how well we know ourselves is imperative in our growth as individuals, with friends, in our families, and with our spouses. Who are we? As a woman of Jamaican descent, I think I can say I have a fair idea of who I am as a black woman. However, if I were to compare myself to others who were born and raised in Jamaica, I do not think I could say that my understanding of my identity is the same.

I know I am not British, but I am also not Jamaican. I am simply a black woman with a British passport whose parents are Jamaicans. I speak two different tongues on a daily basis. One is the workplace etiquette, this tongue speaks to appease the ears of her co-workers. The other is the at home and don't care vibe, this tongue is relaxed and does not have to chew its way through stiff upper lips.

It gets confusing.

In Secondary School when it cams to Black History Month, we would be shown Roots during our History Lessons. On top of that, we were never taught anything about Black British History and always focused on American Black History. It's as though the system was created to stop us from associating ourselves with anyone great, thus, keeping us down.

I'm not saying there is anything wrong with learning

about Malcolm X and Harriet Tubman. What I am saying is this; to deny someone access to history lessons to which they could connect, is to teach them that they do not belong. When you tell someone that they do not belong, you tell them they have no place in your society.

Would you be surprised if I say this is the history of the imposter syndrome that we face as Blacks? We fear our worth because we were taught that no-one cared to show us that we are capable of achieving. If we would have been taught about Olaudah Equiano who, though oppressed for years, was able to buy his freedom, return to England from America and work towards empowering blacks, and became a figure in the anti-slavery movement, maybe then we would be able to feel confident enough to work towards being the best we can be.

This lack has trickled down to younger generations as they have parents who barely know their history. Growing up in a Jamaican household, I learnt about the heroes and heroines of Jamaica amongst many other things, including the motto, the national anthem and the national pledge. The lessons learnt taught me that I didn't have to settle for less and I shouldn't allow injustices to deter me from becoming great. For these young people whose parents are unable to teach them, they will continue to fail to understand that they can be better.

Then there are those living in areas of deprivation; areas where no-one has been able to come out on top. These are the individuals who live to survive. A lot of these guys from 'ends' don't know what it is like to dream and how can they? Who has ever taught them? History lessons empower young girls, thanks to Emmeline Pankhurst and fellow suffragettes. But one, she wasn't black, and two, what about the guys?

For this, and my understanding, I am blessed to be able to do the job I do. I suggest to parents that they research great Black British figures in addition to those from their heritage, educate themselves so they will be able to educate their children. I reinforce the purpose of knowing their history. The purpose of being able to have a historical figure whom they can look up to and aspire to be as great as them or even greater.

We must try to overcome the slave syndrome and the imposter syndrome we have.

Now to go back to the familiarity of splitting tongues. We switch our identity to please others. Classic example? My cousins who grew up in Jamaica. At home, they spoke in fluent patois, on the phone, they spoke with a British accent. They needed to be understood in both lives and in this British life, patois was, and still is, not deemed as good enough. It is seen as uneducated and 'street'. Not good enough for workplaces. Not good enough for this culture.

We do this as Black s, with our slang. Those of us, first or second generation immigrants, acquire words from our parents' mother tongue which intermingles with English. We continually have to remind ourselves that we need to rephrase what we want to say. We can't just say as we wish to others who aren't willing to switch the way they hear things. They get to keep their ears untrained, but we must train our tongues to satisfy their ears.

More often than needs be, we alter our personalities in fear that we will not be accepted. When we step into spaces which are predominantly white, depending on how you were raised and what you are used to, you do begin to feel as though you don't belong.

It's the eyes though. The stares. I've had them. I've been to conferences. All white. Spot the Black. I was an endangered being in a world which set out to kill me, so I felt. No-one wanted to interact with me, no matter how I tried. My hand was ignored on numerous occasions when I had a question. I had to push myself to the front to be able to speak with the organiser.

The craziest thing about all of this Orion, we do this with those we call friends and lovers too. We give them what we assume they want. We project our insecurities and act out our belief system. And this is where it gets messy. By giving them an untrue of us, when we do reveal our authentic self, they get confused and we get angry at them for not accepting the true us.

Why should they? The true us isn't someone they would have wanted to spend time with in the first place. Why should they now accept this version because we initially gave them a different one to work with?

This multi-life we live is nothing but a farce. It stems from us losing ourselves in the chaotic world we live in. It stems from slavery. Our ancestors were forced to remove their cultures and traditions from their lips. They were forced to cut their power. Their slave masters needed to understand what they were saying, so they were forced to be less than.

They needed to conform. They, upon gaining freedom, taught their children to conform. Their children taught their children to do the same. The cycle continued and flowers of deceit and loss of self was tended to perfectly.

Tied tongues kills spirits
Underestimating its power to be free
Opening up to all low frequencies

Hiding behind curtains
Veiled and turbulent
We become victims of ourselves

Unable to correspond with our soul
We allow others to fool us into believing
We are nothing more than expendables

Expanding graves of our selves
Shelving heritages and cultures
Speaking not in the comfort of our hearts

We code-switch
Altering our egos
Utilising our id

We shapeshift our tongues
We strip back ourselves
Destroying our mental

What is freedom when we are still vying for the attention from the oppressors? Yes, we still are oppressed. Subconsciously the white man is still our oppressor. We still view him as having the upper hand. History has taught him that we are still slaves. The struggle continues. We still live in a losing battle.

A battle of regaining one's true identity.

I'm getting hungry though Orion. I must bid you farewell.

With purpose, I'm signing that my crown is cherished.

Niyah Adenike Thomas.

Dear Orton,

Please remind me to call my cousins in Jamaica that London stink. Yes it was good to have the house it was nice but why do people not understand the importance of having a good shower, using deodorant and changing their clothing?

Okay correction, London doesn't stink, too many people in London stink.

To feel the sun on myself was one of the best feelings well I stepped out of my two-bed terraced house with a smile on my face, told my neighbours good morning hope their earphones in. Sauntered to the train station very good mood. Chill and happy.

My 08:02 train came 10 seconds early which wasn't too bad, I was able to slip into one of the window seats. Chittered my body closely to not fill the other commuters.

All was going well until I got to London Bridge station. There were delays on the Jubilee line and the famous foot traffic snaking towards St Thomas' Hospital. Or is it Guys & St Thomas? I'm yet to understand the difference between them, if there is one.

It took me at least 20 minutes to get to the barrier and another 10 minutes to get onto the platform. Technology isn't much of a bad thing, whosoever created wifi was a genius and whomever thought of getting it underground made me thankful I was able to message my line manager and let her know I would be delayed getting in to work. Also took a picture to send to her to prove I wasn't lying. I was only 10 minutes late but still infuriated. Having made my way onto a train, I thought I was going to pass

Dear Orion,

Please remind me to tell my cousins in Jamaica that London stinks. Yes it was good to leave the house. It was nice. But why do people not understand the importance of having a good shower, using deodorant, and changing their clothing?

Okay, correction. London doesn't stink. Too many people in London stink.

To feel the sun on my skin was one of the best feelings yet. I stepped out of my two-bed terraced house with a smile on my face. Told my neighbours good morning. Popped my earphones in. Sauntered to the train station. Very good mood. On time and happy.

My 08:32 train came 30 seconds early which wasn't too bad. I was able to slip into one of the window seats. Clutched my body closely to not hit the other commuters.

All was going well until I got to London Bridge station. There were delays on the Jubilee line and the famous foot traffic snaking towards St. Thomas' Hospital. Or is it Guys & St. Thomas? I'm yet to understand the differentiation between them, if there is one.

It took me at least 20 minutes to get to the barrier and another 10 minutes to get onto the platform. Technology isn't much of a bad thing. Whosoever created Wi-Fi was a genius and whomever thought of getting it underground made me thankful. I was able to message my line manager and let her know I would be delayed getting in to work. Also took a picture to send to her to prove I wasn't lying.

I was only 10 minutes late but still infuriated. Having made my way onto a train, I thought I was going to pass out. It's as though everyone got the *do-not-shower-today* memo except for me. Arms raised above my head. Conversations looming above my 5' stature. The heat underground swelling within the small spaces between bodies.

Why? What did I do to be given the task of dealing with it?

Besides my treacherous journey, I had a wonderful day. One of the best days yet. I had been assigned a young lady on her own, with her three beautiful children. The eldest was no more than 7 years old and the youngest, only 1 years old.

On her face was a tired wiry smile. She was here for help with becoming a better mother for her children. She was in a 10 year relationship with a guy she met in school. They, upon leaving college, had become reacquainted and fell in love.

She thought.

In her words, she had 'been living in a lie and didn't even realise.' He was the first and only guy she was able to forge a romantic relationship with and to see him go, she felt she wouldn't be able to cope, at least she believed it to be so and it became a strain on her.

'I can't believe that we are over.' She said with tears streaming down her face.

'I should have seen it coming. We both began to change. Years ago.'

I listened to her as she spoke. Allowing her the opportunity to share her heart with me. I don't know if she had spoken to anyone in her extended family about this, but I did know that I wouldn't stop her from speaking.

'After the third year in our relationship, I began to feel suffocated. We had our first child then. She was beautiful, still is, and I thought she would help to salvage our relationship. Little did I know, it would make things worse.'

I looked over at her daughter. How precious she was.

Her green eyes glistened and her skin glowed. I could tell that it was her father's eyes which sparkled. A strong gene which he passed unto her.

'Things continued to change. I began reading a lot more about my heritage and was finding myself. He hated it. He told me so.'

I do not know if he was white or of mixed heritage, but it sounded to me that he was not ready for her to delve into herself and wanted to stop her. He knew within himself, whether his conscience was aware of it, that she was discovering her true strength and this made him wary.

He wanted her to run from that which would help her to flourish. He was afraid. She looked at me and smiled a smile of pity, one I was used to seeing from my aunts. One that would feel sorry for my future because I had no idea what it held for me. The pit of my stomach began to open itself up for what would follow.

'I used to wear weaves'. Her eyes didn't leave my hair. 'I wore them because that's what he liked. He loved to be able to run his hand through my hair without meeting any kinks. It reminded him too much of the black women with no class whom he once dated.'

Her hazel eyes glistened as they began to well up. She couldn't have been much older than I, but the wrinkles worn on her forehead spoke for someone who lived their youthful years in a rush. They said she aged suddenly. She needed to be helped out of her mental tragedies.

'I spent hundreds, thousands on hair. I spent hours at the hairdressers.' She shook her head in disbelief. 'I can't believe I allowed him to break down the woman I was to be. The woman I wanted to become.'

'And what woman was that?' I questioned, with notebook in hand, ready to note her response down.

'The black woman who isn't afraid of the world. The one who can be in a relationship with a man from any background while still standing strong for the black community.'

'Now that you are no longer in your long-term relationship, what do you feel you need help with, to be able to move forward as the woman you wanted to be?'

'I need to talk to someone who understands.' She responded as though she was questioning if I understood.

I told her that I understood her and am happy to be here for her to speak to. But, I feel as though I lied to her. Did I really understand? I wear weaves. I spend hours at the hairdressers. I get wigs made up for me. I couldn't attend work without it. I have done so before and was frowned upon.

My hair has become a part of who I am. And there I was, telling a woman who was stuck in a relationship with a man who hated her natural hair that I understood. There I was telling her I understood, yet I knew I wouldn't be able to be as brave as she was. It was at that moment I felt empowered to remove the stitches in my hair. I knew then that I needed to let go of the tracks which oppressed me. The hair which stopped me being my authentic self. The closure which locked me away from freedom. I didn't wear the weaves as a protective style. I wore them to hide who I am. I wore them to please those around me.

The families I work with deserve me being true to myself to be able to speak honestly with them about them doing the same.

My identity is stuck in unbreathable circumstances. It is cut off from the world. I was cut off from it. I have decided that I will remove it. I owe it to myself. I have made a date with myself and on Saturday, I will remove it. This you will hear about. To be able to learn from a client is possibly one of the best things I could have ever done. She brought me back to the peace I had when I left the

house this morning.
    Looks like a good note to leave this entry on. Night Orion.

With purpose, I'm signing that my crown is cherished.

Niyah Adenike Thomas

We all were made to evolve,
To spin on an axis,
Make turning points for ourselves.

We all were made to embrace
Droplets of the sun on our skin,
To glow in its presence.

We all were made to entertain
The peace of the moonlight
Basking in the shower of stars.

We, like the Earth, were made for seasons.
Each season a phase;
Four phases of yearly growth.

Friday 8th August 2019
Time: 23:24

Dear Orion,

I am ecstatic! Nervous but ecstatic. Tomorrow I will be going to buy products for my hair. I have not done this since leaving sixth form.

I grew up embracing my natural hair, or being natural because that's what my parents preferred. I had planned to get my first weave for my 18th birthday so I saved for two years.

As I said, my parents preferred me being natural. My 18th was not going to happen, so I waited until I started university. Researched hairdressers. Spoke to girls I met on my course. I am quite sure I had a vision board at one point. But I got my hair done. I did it.

I, barely a woman, felt like a new woman.

But tonight. This night I know my parents would have loved to witness. Tonight would have been one for the history books. I have managed to return to a state they love. I know I want to love myself too.

Tonight should have been the night I spoke myself out of freeing myself. But my impulse kicked in. Why wait for tomorrow when it could be done tonight? I had no plans to be anywhere.

I removed the shop-bought hair an hour ago. I cried whilst undoing the thread which kept the tracks firmly in place. When I finished, I called Deja and told her. My tears turned to joy. It felt so good.

As I ran my hand through my tresses I began to understand what my client was saying to me yesterday. Her ex's hands were unable to come to terms with the coarseness of her hair. He wanted his experience to be unhindered.

I could feel an unbound nature upon my head. I could feel my ancestors who would have rice, seed, and gold hidden in their hair. I could feel the nature of survival as my hands wandered through my scalp.

I felt disappointment. A sense of disappointment from my ancestors. The men and women who depended on the richness and versatility of the African hair.

I hid my hair because I wanted to be accepted. Now I wanted to make a statement. One which said Niyah Adenike Thomas is growing to be a woman with purpose. One which would prove that I understand what it means to say my crown is cherished.

Work will be different for me from this moment forward. It's okay being a black woman in the office. It's almost a sin being a black woman in bigger meetings. I will be different. I will allow no-one to diminish who I am.

One step closer to being a better me. One step closer to being a continuation of my identity.

I now have work to do and I know this journey will come with blisters like I've never seen before. Blisters I've never had to heal. This is where I will build Niyah Adenike Thomas to be a woman who is unapologetic.

Yet unwarranted sentinels have managed
To take hold of the freedom we knew
Forcing us to stay stuck.

They washed their hands of humanity
As they traded our bodies for currency
A reparation we await today.

But how much will this help?
What can their money give to us
To free my enslaved mind?

I embrace the change which is upon me,

Lingering in my mind,
Seeking a new found freedom.

To be free from their stares
And unburdened by their words
To no longer quiver in their critiques.

I long for the day I quit
Leaving self-sabotage behind
My people need me now more than ever.

I will leave it here for today.

With a new found purpose, I'm signing that my crown IS cherished.

Niyah Adenike Thomas

Dear Orion,

Who would have thought that today would have turned out the way it did?

YouTube + my scarves = a transformed Niyah!

I saw Adam, my neighbour, and he did not recognise me at first. It took him a while to realise the woman before him has been his neighbour for the past 3 years.

I did that!

I found a black-owned hair shop in Lewisham. Yes, black owned. And yes, I still venture into Lewisham. I spoke with the assistant who helped me to find the right type of products for my hair. She directed me to some oils and Shea butter.

I got home. Washed my hair. Gave it a very deep condition. Sang to it as I combed it, giving myself a beautiful head filled with twists.

When I was done, I called my parents via Skype. My mother's eyes, as they do, filled with tears. You would have thought I gave her a grandchild. Nevertheless, I loved her tear filled eyes. They gleamed with pride. She was a proud mother.

My father being my father, sat before the screen giving off little emotion. Shook his head and rubbed his eyes. His words to me, *'welcome back prodigal child'.*

All I could do during that moment was smile.

'Do not cry for my hair.' I said as I ran my hand through it. Clunky twists bounced as my fingers passed them.

'Baby I am crying because you look so beautiful.' Dad rolled his eyes as mum blubbered through her words.

'Dad behave.' I mockingly scolded him.

'I don't always understand the tears Niyah.' He laughed

his heart warming laugh. The one which gave you peace within. He is one of the strongest men I know. I see where Nick gets his strength. It only makes sense.

'You are so beautiful, young Empress.' He meant every word he said. This wasn't one of those moments he would say something to make you feel happy because he didn't want to be the bad guy.

'Thank you Daddy.'

Mum had left for a brief moment, returning with tissues as she dried her face.

'Why the natural hair Niyah? The daughter I know never leaves her natural hair out.'

'I had an epiphany on Thursday when I met with a client, Mum. She made me see that I was fooling everyone and myself.' I didn't tell Mum that this woman gave me the pity eyes I grew so familiar with receiving when I was younger. I did however, tell her that this woman helped me to see who I was. She helped me to realise that I needed to be one with my identity in order to truly be the authentic me my soul craved.

I told you this yesterday Orion. My parents were going to be happy and they didn't prove me wrong when we Skyped.

I wish for a day to speak with them about the incident when I was 18 years old. But I guess one day at a time is what we shall work with.

One day for them to be overjoyed at my return to my nature. One day for my body's history. One day for the family black sheep. One day at a time for each aspect I'd like to talk to them about.

For that moment, I embraced the delight. In that moment, I learned that my mother wasn't too dissimilar from myself. She too had gone through her *impress the world* phase. Her turning point was my father.

They met on a day she thought she looked her worst.

To him, however, that was her best. She wore no makeup, her hair was bare, her skin flushed with sweat. She was running through Hyde Park early morning before she would go to her hairdresser for yet another weave.

Dad saw before him a woman unimpeded by society's expectations. She wasn't the woman he thought she was though. She cloaked her insecurities in makeup and false hair so she could feed the cravings of the world of which she was a part.

He did discover later, that she didn't always walk around with the Black Panther mentality. As he saw her in her natural state, he thought there was room for her to open up and venture out into her insecurities. Be vulnerable enough for others to understand that she was happy as she was.

It made sense as to why she was never completely against my wearing a weave, but I wish I had known this story of her hair when I was much younger.

I do appreciate only finding this out though. I have had the opportunity to go through my moments of weakness where I felt obliged to be accepted for my conformity. I have felt how painful it is to live with an unresolved burden. Coming out on the other side is a blessing.

Mum's story was there to help with guiding my steps that I would have to take, a rock to stand on in the coming days and months where my hair will create a shift within my workplace.

I accept and appreciate everything that has come before. I am not everything which happened to me. I am the woman who has not been broken. I'll leave it here today.

With a new found purpose, I'm signing that my crown IS cherished.

Niyah Adenike Thomas

Dear Orion,

Time to make the most of my day. It is H O T outside! I will not complain, but it is so hot!

My plan for the day is this:

o Take a trip to the gym
o Find something to do with the wigs and other hair that I own
o Do my monthly shopping
o COOK
o Find an updo for my mane
o Head over to my parents' house for Sunday dinner

Doesn't look like a hectic list, but I know it's going to be a lot to get through. The most challenging thing today I think will be the dinner at my parents' house.

I know that my hair will be something new for my siblings, nephews, nieces, aunts, uncles and even grandparents. Everyone has grown accustomed to seeing me with hair I bought. My sister has taken digs at me about it before, so I can't see today being any different.

I am nervous. I cannot lie to you about that at all. To lie to you would mean I am trying to lie to myself. Not possible.

My siblings and I are still in contact with each other, but our relationship isn't the greatest. I do however have a wonderful relationship with their children. Charlene has twin sons and a daughter, while Nick has a daughter.

The thing about my siblings is though we may not have the greatest relationship, they have done something for their children which our aunts and mum did for us when growing up; introduce them to me. Over the years I'd take them for a weekend and spend time with them.

We either went to the cinema or to a book shop for children. We'd go to museums or just stay in my house and cook or bake.

I loved having them over.

They are the ones we couldn't be while growing. I haven't made the mistake made by my grandparents, telling each of them the meaning of their names and dictating that they should portray its meaning through their actions.

I do not think they are at an age where they are mature enough to access life's philosophy. I want to give them the space to remain as children. To be young and free. Also, I don't want to use myself as an example, that would do more harm than it would good.

The way I feel mentally, it's as though spring has come around once again. I'm ready for a new start. Ready to take this world on by storm. This woman who has been fearful before, is now ready to be her bold self.

The bold I was unable to be when in primary school.

I guess it's going to be a very short one from me today Orion. If I stay any longer I won't be able to make it through my to-do list.

With a new found purpose, I'm signing that my crown IS cherished.

Niyah Adenike Thomas.

Dear Orion,

Today, Charlene and I had a long conversation. I called her during my lunch break as my throat erupted from being stuffed with stifled tears. I sputtered through words as I tried to explain to my sister that my day was everything perfectly correct yet my emotions could not match up with how I had planned to handle the pre-empted stares and whispers.

We met up at one of the pubs in Forest Hill after work. My eyes were no longer the puffy red they were after lunch. At work I lied and said that it was because they were irritated and frantic rubbing caused the swell. I told everyone I didn't think to visit the pharmacy to buy myself a bottle of eyedrops for it. My white lie allowed them to focus on the human me as opposed to my hair for at least ten minutes.

Charlene was affectionate. Something I rarely saw in her. Her affection is frequently given to everyone but me. This was a moment to embrace.

'Hunny, these things happen and you yourself said you knew it would.' She lifted her glass to her lips. The dark red liquid swirled within as she tilted it to allow it to slip into her mouth.

Charlene is beautiful. She dismisses negativities to allow herself to focus and it heightens her glow. I had never noticed it before now. There were no bags under her eyes - even with children and the job she did, she still managed to get enough rest. She had a chestnut complexion, warm brown finish and a red undertone. My sister is beautiful. Her height suits her personality. She is 5'9. Not too short, but not too tall.

I couldn't do much more than sigh.

'You will not be accepted if you do not have something which resembles them. You will never be white, and our hair terrifies them.'

I guess she was right, but it didn't stop me from feeling the way I felt.

'It's a life we have to learn to navigate our way through. What you did all these years was to adjust in order to have an easier pass in society, but how did it really pan out for you? Think about your mental wellbeing, how's that been for you? Did your hair really make things better for you? Do you even know what it is you have been running away from all this time?'

I listened to my sister for the first time and understood everything she was saying to me. Our conversation continued and I can't tell you how much of an insight I got.

From feeling disappointed with the way I handled myself at work, to feeling embarrassed to have to lean on my sister, I can't tell you how much better I feel about everything right now.

To have allowed Charlene into my mind has given me the opportunity to ponder. I had thoughts racing across my mind as I was on my way home. What stuck out to me was how much my childhood has had an impact on me over the years.

I spent years trying to hide myself. I can't help but think that if things were different, I would not have had this new reality to learn to deal with. Had I understood life then as I did now, I would have chosen to forgive those involved in moulding me to be who I am today rather than suppressing the feelings to my own detriment.

This list of those whom I'd forgive begins with none other than me. I am the one to be held accountable. I have yet to forgive Jah and Ricardo. When it comes to

Ricardo I think it will be much more difficult for me to forgive him, but one day I'd love to be able to do so; I'd need to release my hang ups that I have about him. I can say I forgive my siblings, parents, aunts, uncles, and grandparents too.

They don't know the role they have played in my detrimental descent, but I do want to be able to move on and embrace life in the way I should.

I guess I can start my steps towards forgiveness here, in this present moment.

Unintentional and without spite,
You have forced my bows to break.
I too afraid refused to stand straight,
Allowed you to be a tornado
When only slight dust you would blow.

Dear Jah, we were young,
Yet my confidence you stole.
Dear Ricardo, still young for foresight
But my innocence you stole.
Dear Charlene and Nick
I was always unable to understand
The hate my siblings would show.
Dear aunties and uncles,
Your wisdom was never applied,
You played such a huge role.
Dear mum and dad,
Where were you when I needed my heroes?
Dear mama and papa,
You thought it was for the best but little did you know.
Dear Niyah,
You made your choices,
You knew what was wrong,
You wrote your story.

Dear all,
I have forgiven you.
I have chosen peace.
I can only accept love with a pure heart.
I trust me with my decisions.
I cannot allow for the past to be my driving factor,
If my actions are steered into the wrong direction.

From this point forward
I can only look within for guidance,
I appreciate the lessons I have learnt from you all.
This I know will not be easy,
But I am ready for change.
I am ready for the demons I will face,
Those ready to stop me,
I am open to fight against them
Rather than allow them to tear me down.

The sunset will be my new favourite place, Orion. It is the release of all things good and bad. The end of horrors and beginning of sobriety. To mirror its blessing is one I hope others can recognise in me, the portal of peace.

And here we are. In clarity, a place I wish I was during work today. All is not lost, tomorrow is a new day. I can try again. Tomorrow, I will be able to work towards walking with my head held high. I can't stop the stares, but I can control my confidence. When I did my shopping yesterday, I was bold. I was confident in my strides. It does not have to be saved for shopping trips.

Now the sun has begun to go down, I will allow the negative emotions brought up today to fade away. It's not a burden I wish to carry with me for another day. With each day going forward I wish to undo layers of myself.

I will use the time to uproot any weeds which have stifled parts of me. The first place I wish to begin; letting go of Kyron. He serves no purpose in the betterment of myself. I cannot progress if I keep him close to my heart.

He may have been for booty call purposes which serves sexual gratification only. Well, that's a thought for a different day.

I think you know what's going to happen now right?

It's time I say goodnight.

To see my thoughts before my eyes have been uplifting. So thank you for being here to allow me to share my inner thoughts with you.

With a new found purpose, I'm signing that my crown IS cherished.

Love,

Niyah Adenike Thomas.

Dear Orion,

Today's been good thus far. I'm currently very bored in the office. I've had two meetings and written up my notes, leaving my calendar empty for the rest of the day. Quite frankly, I do not feel like doing much else, hence, today's earlier acquaintance.

I met with the Agyepongs this morning and I can't tell you how pleased I am to find out about their progress. There was something much different about them today. Their love shone through in a way I had never seen before. I have been working with them for over a year now and am proud to see how far they have come.

Mrs Agyepong mentioned the work they have done as a family on affirmations. Having had the time to discuss their pasts and truly listen to each other, they started to find a middle ground in their relationship and was moving towards a better equilibrium.

It amazes me that there are individuals in relationships who have not yet learnt how to communicate effectively. This lack has stopped them growing and prevented them becoming the couple they longed to be. Some 'accidentally' ended up in relationships, just because.

If this is not addressed, their children become victims of their toxicity, contributing to the negative teachings passed on to second generations. However, this isn't to say there aren't children who have become adults and chosen not to repeat their parent's behaviours. It seems like you either repeat their mistakes or do the complete opposite.

As well as the Agyepongs, I met with a new client who

called himself broken. His eyes loitered on the floor for most of the session. He, I know, has a long way to go. Another black man from a single parent home. Another black man who had no idea he'd managed to make it past the age of 21, let alone be a father now.

He was emotionally unavailable in the beginning, but when she got pregnant, he thought it would be best for them both to move in together. Little did he know this would be a mistake he would grow to regret and it would cause him to face much turmoil.

I spent the time observing his body language and saw how much he curled in on himself when he spoke about the mother of his child. It was painful to watch. He won't be someone I can assess or draw conclusions about in one session. There are some individuals whom I can assess within a session, but he was different. I could tell.

What is it about us which forces us to sabotage ourselves? I understand that our past relationships and experiences play a part in this, but it still puzzles me.

I listened to him as he spoke. Beating himself up throughout the session. He was a victim to himself which was very difficult to listen to.

Something about him was very familiar. His disposition saddened me and I really wanted to cry for him. I am quite certain that this has nothing to do with my period which is just around the corner. Things shifted when he got in the room.

The atmosphere changed.

Honestly, I should have had the meeting in one of the meeting rooms, but instead, I chose to remain in my office.

He wouldn't stop repeating, 'I'm broken... I'm a broken man.'

He, James, was so convinced that he was broken and needed to be fixed as opposed to being hurt and needed to heal.

    What I wish could have been said in that meeting was -
    What is your identity?
    Do you know where you belong?
    Can you tell me your position in society?

    Cold icy bars were not made to keep you locked in,
    Yet you continuously mess up to be judged
    Having people predict your future to be behind bars.

    The streets were not to be your home,
    Yet you chose to be fathered by a fatherless generation
    And leave your mother worried to death

    It is time you look within yourself to see your worth,
    Identify your strengths and be the Black King you ought to be,
    Leading the weak to freedom from their oppressed minds.

    Your ancestors walked miles and fought fights,
    They hunted and protected,
    Not for you to settle for less.

    Why are you still sleeping child?
    Why have your goals been put aside?
    Why do you no longer try?

    You have the potential to be the world's greatest!
    Stop preventing your own success;
    Be the man you ought to be.

You must stop living in the shadows of your
fears.
Recognise that you are great
With greatness to be achieved.

Black King,
You have an empire to rule
With people who will look up to you.

Black King,
Believe you can
And go for it!

Black King,
Step up to the challenges life throws at you
And work your way to the top.

Stand in front of the mirror,
Look yourself in your eyes
And say

You are handsome.
You're a boss.
I am special.
I am a KING.

I will indeed implement affirmations in the sessions,
and I guess that would need to run hand in hand in helping him to unearth his identity.

I'm getting a call Orion, I'll either come back tonight
or you will see me here tomorrow.

So, with a new found purpose, I'm signing that my crown
IS cherished.

Niyah Adenike Thomas.

Wednesday 13th August 2020
Time: 11:00

Does it even matter today?

Wednesday 13th August 2020
Time: 13:20

Dear Orion,

I should not be doing this, but why not? I am sitting in a stuffy meeting with executives speaking about things not pertaining to me. The agenda has been ignored and quite frankly, I am not interested in what they have to speak about.

Team Building Day! Yay! Whatever, right? Why would I want to torture myself by being amongst those who hate me?

Wednesday 13th August 2020
Time: 21:00

Dear Orion,

I am grateful.

I am blessed.

I am always growing.

I am proud of me.

I start with this because though today was difficult, I am still able to come back to you with a clear mind. Affirmations work.

I received an email from my manager asking to speak with me about how I present myself around the office. In other words, my hair was a misrepresentation. I then had to sit in a meeting knowing that I was an 'offence' and all being said had nothing to do with me.

I spent most of the day trying to pick myself up as everything felt wrong. Everything with me was wrong, for them.

It took me some time to gather myself, but I did it and I am proud of my strength and resilience to push through.

So, let's start with my manager.

She felt the need to call me into her office, summon me into her office to be more precise, because I wasn't upholding the dress code, one of which I had no awareness.

A dress code which didn't mind when I wore jeans to work.

The tone of her email already had me fuming, which inadvertently led to my heart already feeling as if it was boiling over as I walked into her office. She had the most beautiful yet insincere smile. She had the nerve to start with small talk, ask how my week was thus far and how my appointments were coming along.

I smiled as I mentally reminded myself that I ought to breathe. 'My week has been wonderful, thank you Sandra.' I had answered, my face unbothered, my energy unwelcoming.

To kill time and extend the awkward air in her office, she peered over the rim of her glasses as she tapped away at the keyboard.

'You wanted to speak to me about my dress code Sandra?' I couldn't sit there and allow time to fill the space we were in. I would have rathered allowing my thoughts to drown time as I pondered every reason as to why I couldn't find love.

'Yes'. She stopped and looked over at me. Point to Sandra for acknowledging me I guess.

'Well, it's not so much your dress code, but as I mentioned in the email, there have been complaints and disgruntled talks about your new –' she paused as though she were waiting for me to complete her sentence. One thing with our job, we never fill the gap with our own thoughts when we see our clients, so I didn't see why I would have done that for her. My eyes stared out at her.

I couldn't bring myself to change the way I felt.

'Your new look. Your hair has been mentioned on several occasions as unprofessional.'

I smiled at her. I knew what would come next would be a shock to her system but I needed her to wake up. I needed her to understand that there was no way I would allow her to bring me down for something so natural.

'Sandra, you and I have been working in this office for long enough, therefore, I know you are aware that the hair of others has never been an issue.' I sat up in my chair and leaned forward. I wanted her to feel uncomfortable as I spoke. Manager or not, I would not allow her to force me into thinking I am to play second best.

Lowering my voice, I continued. 'I may lose my job for saying this, but I want you to know, just because you are happy to sit back and play dress-up for the Caucasians in this office and those who are executives, doesn't mean I will allow you to demean me.'

Despite the tornado that had been brewing within me since reading her email, I suddenly felt at peace.

I proceeded. 'My sister said something to me on Monday. Remember that day my eyes were puffy? Well, that day, I met with my sister. She is older than I am, and she said something I believe will stick with me forever. You will not be accepted if you do not have something which resembles them. You will never be white and our hair terrifies them. In other words, you and I do not have a white skin and there is nothing in our DNA which will allow for that to happen. You and I, no matter what will never be accepted by them because we can never be white. To top it off, our hair terrifies them. I am happy to continue to push them into the depths of their fears when they look at me. You can refer to me as Medusa.'

Sandra was shocked.

She didn't interject when I spoke and I was getting ready to go back to my office and begin packing as I felt sure she would have given me a dismissal, effective immediately.

Here, at work, I learn life lessons and to have had a client who was able to force me into thinking was one of the most beautiful things I could have asked for. I was mentally enslaved by thinking I needed to have been accepted by my colleagues by wearing weaves.

I finished up what I was saying to Sandra and still in her state of mental incapability to speak with reason, she smiled and said thanks.

As freeing as that moment was, I had to get to a meeting with everyone who felt as though I was being offensive towards them. Can you believe it? My hair was threatening to them and I wasn't seen as professional. I guess I reminded them of what slaves looked like when their forefathers owned plantations.

I purposely ensured I was able to make an entrance, so waited until the last minute to enter into the meeting room. Budget meetings barely held my interest and today I didn't feel as though I needed to be very cordial with my attitude.

As I walked in, all eyes went to my hair. I, the talk of the office, was there, living proof before them. I took a seat, pulled my notebook out, pulled you out, and began to attempt to write. I past calm and into infuriated.

The Chief Executive would not stop staring at my hair. This was the same from everyone else also. I was truly a distraction. The meeting happened, with very many pauses. And, the thing I almost failed to tell you, I sat at the front.

Yes, I sat at the front. Had you out and was trying to write notes to you.

There were moments during the meeting where I was asked questions in very simple and basic ways, as though the loss of the straight hair had removed my inability to continue doing what I needed to do.

My client list needed to be increased and, for some reason, 'diversified'. Will this stop me from going to work with my hair loud and proud? Not at all.

I have never worn bold colours to work when it comes to my hair, but am now tempted to do so just to bring home the point. There are two members of staff here, Nicky and Jennifer, who have dyed their hair purple. Both of these ladies are whites, and neither have been pulled up on their hair.

I know this because I am an assistant manager and everyone speaks their business loud enough for you to live vicariously through them.

All of that being said, I am grateful for this day and the

openness of my colleagues' disgust towards me worn on their faces.

My hair is the crown I have been failing to embrace.

And I thank them all for being discriminatory.

Tomorrow, I will deal with my caseload because I refuse to be forced out of my job.

Now, I will love and leave you.

With a new found purpose, I am signing that my crown IS cherished.

Niyah Adenike Thomas.

Thursday 14th August 2019
Time: 20:07

Dear Orion,

Today was a better day, but client wise, it was difficult. I met with James once more today, and to listen to a man who has no sense of identity is much more difficult than being called into an office about my hair.

James works in a bank, one he wouldn't disclose, but said he was satisfied there. As a father, he mentioned he was afraid that he wouldn't be enough for his child and he was interested in going to university to further himself in a course which holds his interest.

Though he has thought about it, he has been afraid of doing so because he doesn't want to fail. He has no qualifications past his A-levels and is genuinely afraid that he will not be able to access what he would be taught.

Additionally, he was afraid of rejection and that being said, he found it difficult to complete the application.

He found that it was natural for him to procrastinate and possibly miss opportunities, rather than fail during an attempt

He reminded me of everyone I have ever met, myself included. We all want to achieve, but on our journey towards success we fail by yielding to procrastination. Procrastination morphs into laziness and then shape shifts itself to the final stage, quitting.

'I remember being smart in school.' He smiled faintly.

'Didn't have to study much for exams. Teachers loved me.' He inhaled deeply. 'This was before GCSEs.'

We were hit with silence. Not the awkward type. More of the silence which made you think. The silence filled with questions that would never be asked and statements that would never be said.

'It's amazing how much damage school can do to you. I was always at the top of my class. Always did what I had to do. Always got my homework done on time. Always passed my exams with flying colours. Never got in trouble. Always kept my head down. Until I got to Year 9. That's when everything changed.'

He stood. His eyes vacant.

'Why did things change in Year 9? What happened?'

This is the part of my job which crossed over with psychology. The need to understand my clients to then be able to help them accordingly. For some clients, I refer them to our counselling team, others, I'm able to work with them without intervention. I couldn't tell if James required intervention, but I knew I needed to listen to him.

'I was being shut out of the groups I wanted to be part of. I needed to be a different person in order to fit in.' He paced around my office. 'I stopped putting the work in. Started going home late. I stopped caring.' As I listened to him, I was able to understand him some more.

It's a shame to know this is how some of our men lost themselves; a result of some not having had a father, or a good enough male role model to have discussions with, about being a man and the importance of being true to oneself despite the sneers from others.

It doesn't help that the world we live in prevents parents from spending quality time with their children. Children spend approximately 6 hours at school, in lessons only, then there are after school clubs which tend to be between 30 minutes and an hour. This doesn't include the time taken for them to travel to and from school.

When it comes to children in Primary school, if parents have no other option, they may have to get a childminder to take their child to and from school, as they need to get to and from work themselves. This means they may only see their child at breakfast and briefly at dinner before they need to do homework and head to bed.

Children in Secondary school may not see their parents as much as they tend to be more independent and parents may give them more 'breathing room'. Breakfast, if the child does have breakfast, may not be together, and dinner may only be eaten in their room. With more homework to be done, they may be shut away a lot more than before.

All this to say, we lose contact time with our children, the older they become.

This system has been in place for some years and it has not changed. And when you think about it, coming from a single parent home, with no support from other family members, and the males you see around aren't the best examples, it's very easy to lose yourself.

James lost himself. It is my job to help him to regain his connection with his inner power. I found it difficult in myself to stop looking at him as though he were a project to be fixed. Over the years, Marcel taught me that people didn't need to be fixed, but instead, needed a helping hand to be healed. At this moment, James looked more and more like a broken artefact. I wanted to fix him, but Marcel's voice wouldn't allow me to.

Orion, can I really help this man as I should? Is it possible for me to guide him to healing?

Well, it's that time for me to say good night. I think this is a good place for me to leave it. I may return to James one day, but won't promise that it will be tomorrow.

With a new found purpose, I am signing that my crown IS cherished.

Niyah Adenike Thomas.

Dear Orion,

There are men like Marcel who know their worth and truly care for and respect women. There are men like James who struggle to find worth in themselves, yet still have respect for women.

Then there are those other men. The men who do not know how to take hints. The men who are very pushy and crave attention. The men who are sexually demeaning, but do not think they are doing anything wrong.

These are the men who continually give all men a bad name. The things they do and the way they come off to women leaves us with a terrible taste in our mouths. We want to love our Black Men, but it's difficult when the ones who cross paths with us are those who need to work on themselves. Because of them, the good guys, the ones who really want to treat us well, shy away from approaching us because they care. The fact they care, they try not to put us in the same predicament these good-for-nothing men put us in. I really wanted to use a different word, but there was nothing else I could say.

I met this type of good-for-nothing man today. I was on my lunch break and he took it upon himself to sit with me. With all other tables free, he chose to sit around the same table with me and it made no sense whatsoever.

Before I go too far with this, let me set the scene for you. There is a food court close to where I work with an array of restaurants. Not only is it close to where I work, but also to where he works; we are two doors apart. It's not my first time visiting this restaurant and not my first time seeing him either.

He isn't a bad looking guy, but our interaction was just

enough for me to never want to see him again.

I walked into my usual Italian lunchtime restaurant, Mamma in Cucina, and as always, the greetings I received were beautiful and warm. I engaged in the typical small talk with Eleonora, one of the waitresses, as I placed my order. Today felt different, so I trusted my feelings and changed my order, a little shock to Eleanora. She had already memorised my every day order and had been ready to put it through until I stopped her.

As it's not a restaurant you have to wait to be seated in, I chose to sit at a table in the far back corner. I wanted to be away from it all today, so found that it was the perfect place to sit. I wanted to give my mind the opportunity to rest and indulge in the silence it was missing.

I was happy and content to be alone, for the brief moment it lasted.

Then in he came.

What I can't understand is this; it's a restaurant, there are vacant tables, yet you choose to sit with me. I am quite certain that I am not as inviting as he made it seem, thus my confusion. He smiled a creepy smile at me and had I not been comfortable where I was, I would have packed my things and got up.

'How has your day been?' I heard him ask. With my nose deep in a book, I pretended not to hear him. Acted as though I was off in my own zone.

Unfortunately, he was unable to take the hint and instead lightly touched the back of my hand. I took a deep breath, closed my eyes for a second before looking up at him.

I tried to give the blankest look I could muster up. 'Yes?'

There was the smile again. Something about it was very sketchy. 'How has your day been?'

'Fine.' And I returned to my book. I didn't want to

participate in a conversation with him, or anyone else as a matter of fact. 'What have you been up to? I don't see much of you these days.'

'Sir, I'm trying to enjoy a book. I don't want a conversation. I just want to allow my mind to decompress.'

I took another deep breath before placing my eyes where they needed to be, in my book.

'You know you don't need to be rude right?' He asked. I ignored.

'And you wonder why Black Men don't want to date Black Women.' He bit.

I continued to ignore him, my blood beginning to boil.

'A man tries to speak to you and all you do is get rude and ignore him. I'm just trying to have a conversation with you.'

'Look.' I spat. 'You were not invited to sit here. I did not initiate a conversation of any sort with you. Of all the seats, you placed yourself here. You cannot be mad that I do not want to speak with you.'

I looked deeply into his eyes and saw my cousin. The manipulation was there. Ricardo was the soul I saw before me. I know not all men were like this, but at that moment, I saw my cousin. All fangs and poison. This man, whose name I had never known and will never learn, was ready to drain my soul.

'It wouldn't kill you to be polite though, would it?' He asked.

As if on cue, Eleonora came over with my dish. 'I have another table free if you want.' I smiled at her request and told her thanks. I was not willing to sit at a table with someone who wanted to gaslight me and give me indigestion. Let's not go there with the self-sabotage. Not today, or any day as a matter of fact.

I would love to give my love to a Black Man, but some of them make it difficult to do so. There is that, and the fact that manipulation leads to me having flash-backs of a past which led to me hating many men. That is just for me, what about for the other Black Women who have for years been raped, disowned by their families, sold to sex trades, been physically abused by their partners?

When there are men who believe they have the right to say anything and not be frowned upon or reprimand-ed, it's difficult for us to give in to love? Another reason many of us would prefer to be in situationships.

For example, right now, the person I'd rather be with this minute is Kyron. Though there is nothing between us, relationship wise, I do miss being held by him. I miss our bodies collapsing together. Where we aren't com-mitted to each other, it makes everything easier. It does defeat my wanting to fall in love though, doesn't it?

Mind you, I do think tonight could be a night I call him once again.

I think I should leave this one here tonight. I'll let you know if and when I next meet with him.

For now though, with a new found purpose, I am signing that my crown IS cherished.

Niyah Adenike Thomas.

If we were so precious
Would it not make sense
If we were handled with care?
Would it not make sense
If we were not gaslighted?

If we were so precious
Would it not be smart
For us to be looked after?
If these men who were to be our Kings
Were to stop wasting our time
And honoured us?

Is it wrong that I prefer quick moments of lust,
As opposed to attempting what could be
Years of love?

What are the steps I'd need to take
To remove myself from such?
What more can I do
To become a better woman for myself?

I know to be considered better,
I must view myself as rare,
But what if I'm unsure of how
How to let go of my own traumas?

What if he has traumas of his own
Do I forgive him unknowingly?
Or do I walk on by
Head held above traumas defeat?

Saturday 16th August 2019
Time: 10:00am

Dear Orion,

It's insane to think how much we value our Black Men in comparison to our Black Women. I have found that my conversations as of late have been about the way Black Women are treated, and it's led me to think about this; what is it this that stops society from giving Queens the voice we truly deserve? We are expected to be strong warriors, but when we experience injustice we quietly fight for them.

A book by Robin Walker, 'When We Ruled' actually talks about the days women were treated as true Royalty. Our presence was valued. We were pillars, and still are, but in today's world, we don't seem to be missed when gone.

Could this be a result of us all being brainwashed?

If Black Women are portrayed as hoodrats, bitches, and breeding grounds, could this be the reason we are not missed? What needs to happen for us to not be seen as expendables?

It's incredibly insane how difficult it is for the Black Woman but we still try to fight for our Black Men.

When will we normalise fighting for our Black Women?

How many of our Queens are wrongly incarcerated?

How many of our Queens are being sexually assaulted because 'they asked for it'?

How many of our Queens have lost their children at birth because they were denied the proper treatment?

How many of our Queens have underlying illnesses because doctors refuse to send them into the hospital for tests to be carried out?

How many of our Queens have lost their dignity be

cause they've been paraded around for the gratification of johns? We've been through, and are still going through, myriads of torments. While this is the case, we are still expected to stay strong and be the pillar for our men, community, family, and the younger generation.

I've never known poison to taste this good.
Its inhibition too comfortably clings to cells,
Latches to all senses
Sensitivity removed.
We are now renowned for being
The addition in a matrix of jarred souls,
Pieces of us being chipped off.
We aren't chips off the old block,
We are the whole block broken down,
Our chips taken as tokens
And no matter how battered we present in the present
They still fail to believe us.

Would you miss me if I was no longer here?
Would you beat doors down until my truth was freed?
Would you march with thousands behind you, rallying for my justice?
Would you?
Would you petition so no other woman would face discrimination from healthcare professionals?
Would you?

Poison has become the sun bathed in during winter,
Leaving burns penetrated deeply into the mental,
Soaring into the muddied world now home to

lack of empathy
Girdling a nation obesely grotesque,
Having indulged in the theft of our minds and
bodies
As we fight to keep our souls.

What more are we without souls?
Orion, this world is unfair.
When men honestly care and show it, they are made fun of. Ever hear the word simping? Neither did I, not until today. Seeing it in a sentence got my attention. The placement of the word made me find its definition. Supposedly, it's to do with when a man places 'too much' value on a woman.
Can you imagine? Too much value. Too much value? I'm intrigued to find out how this is measured.
Reminds me of the days I heard men being told they were 'whipped' because they showed they cared. These thoughts have become the norm which had not been challenged prior to, well, I'm not sure if they have been challenged ever, scrutinised, crucified.
There's a part within me which believes it must have already been challenged. I fail to believe, within today's world, that no-one has begun to make noise about these things.
Questions are already loitering, asking why Kings fail to treat Queens well, especially those from homes with single mothers. This has to mean that the words spoken reinforce negative attitudes towards women who are being attacked.
We need our men to feel free and comfortable in treating their women well.
The mixed messages are nothing but sickening.
On the one hand we would love for men to be more communicative, more emotional, more understanding,

more of everything positive. On the other, they are weak and defined comparatively as female genital regions, referencing cats, to be more specific, a pussy.

To tell a man he is a little girl, or even being a bitch is to say women's emotions are of no relevance in its own subtle way.

Goes to show that it's not only what is said to women that brings us down, but it's also the negative references made including us. To say a man talks too much for a man, is saying only women should talk a lot, in some sense. It also hints that to speak a lot is a bad thing, which tells a woman to reduce how frequently she shares her words. If we aren't careful, we will force her into retracting sentences before they are spoken, pushing her into mutism

When will we assess and evaluate the value placed on our Black Women?

I know I'm asking these questions to you and you are only my notebook, but I guess by seeing them will push me towards action, I hope.

It would be wonderful if I could get support from work to publicly show we provide a safe space for Black Women. Even better if I could encourage them to have group sessions for Black Women only. You and I know, however, that will be difficult due to previous conversations I've had with Miss Kiss-Ass about my hair.

I'm going to leave it here tonight Orion.

With a new found purpose, I am signing that my crown IS cherished.

Niyah Adenike Thomas.

Love in Black

Sunday 17th August 2019
Time: 11:27am

Dear Orion,

Upon reflection, I've been smiling. You've taken on a lot of my trauma, my stress, and pain through your pages over the past couple of months and I thank you. By talking to you, I've come to understand a lot about myself, my family, friends, colleagues, and society.

When thinking about myself, the choices I've made or my reactions to things, I've understood in greater depths the role my unresolved childhood traumas had.

My family hated me because my grandparents placed such high value on me.

Saying that, I didn't tell you about the meeting we had! I'll pause here just to allow for us to rewind to that night.

Awkward does not describe or define how it was for the first 15-20 minutes.

No-one uttered a word to me. No-one except my siblings and Mishika, a cousin who is approximately 4 years older than I am.

The glances shot in my direction were sharp enough to split steel.

I felt as though the 7 year old me had paid an unexpected visit. She comfortably placed discomfort in my body, all the while feeding anxiety to my heart and mind. The shock of her surprise visit force fed anaesthetic to my muscles. All of my mental preparation was disregarded.

'Why did you bother coming, Niyah?' She asked. 'You know they hate you.'

I tried to brush my younger self's words aside, greeted my grandparents and took a seat around the table. That's when Mishika spoke to me. To be honest, I couldn't remember her from my childhood, but apparently she was around.

'Hey Niyah.' She smiled as she pulled a chair out to sit down.

Her smile looked genuine which was surprising to me. It's very rare I'd receive a genuine and authentic smile from one of Mum's family members.

'Hey' I replied, strained, as I couldn't think of her name immediately.

She noticed and smiled another smile. 'It's Mishika' she said. 'I'm Jah's sister. You wouldn't have noticed me because I was always minding my own business being a loner.'

I'm quite sure I almost choked when she mentioned Jah's name.

'My brother was a jackass back in the day.' She continued, reminding me of the day he told me no-one liked me.

'Some of it was a result of what we heard at home.' Her eyes averted themselves to her hands. 'My mum was very manipulative. I wanted to talk to you because you seemed cool, but I knew my mum would have had a heart attack had I done so.'

A lump formed in the back of my throat. This was the first time in twenty-eight years I was given any insight into why Jah told me no-one liked me and why he said he hated me. The raging bull, born from years of mistreatment, had awoken but had not been angered. Instead, I felt the healing occurring.

I must say, this is what I strongly believe in when working with my families: Adults are a product of their childhood. Unresolved toxic children produce harmful adults. Healed teenagers produce healthy adults. It's difficult for this to be normalised though. You can't normalise something if you're unaware of unresolved traumas to work through.

With this in mind, I try to ensure the families I work with work towards doing well for their children. It's always important for parents to do right for the wellbeing of their children.

'Why Jah has never spoken to you since is beyond me.' Mishika continued. 'Though that being said, it's taken me this long to talk to you.'

Mishika's honesty was endearing.

'It did take me some years to unlearn the misguidance of my mother's pain.'

I listened to her and noticed something, she spoke with a London accent, not what I would expect from Jah's sibling.

'When did you move back to London?'

Her smile was heavy and I could tell there would be more to her answer. Fortunately for her, she was saved by Papa. I, to this day can't believe Jah had a sister I knew nothing about.

Being at my grandparents' house was a painful nostalgia.

Now all adults with our own definitions of familial love and many unresolved issues, the meeting had us all in very bad ways.

'All of you want to carry grudges but don't even know why!' Papa started.

'Yuh parents put this on each of you since you did likkl.' He continued. 'But why yuh carry them to this day is what I don't understand.'

He may not have understood, but I did. Having never been reprogrammed to think differently, we carried on in the ways we knew. Some would argue that as adults we should know better. An argument which stands well on its own, but there are factors; external factors that always play a huge role in an adult's outlook and the actions they choose to take.

'Some of you don't even realise the power you have and the greater power of your names. Yuh parents tell yuh that me and yuh grandmother love Niyah more and what did you do?'

Looking around, everyone seemed to wear the discomfort I felt. Something I was feeling in the moment, once again, having the spotlight on me. Another reason for the hatred to continue right?

The problem here was that Papa was pinning the blame on our parents, my cousins, and siblings, leaving himself, my grandmother, and I out of it.

It's an omission I was familiar with when working with some families. No-one wants to take blame, so they allow projection to intrude as they pin blame on others. It's a case of being at peace with yourself and understanding your downfalls before being able to include yourself in the wrongs you've contributed to.

'Papa may I just say something?' I interjected. Unsure of whether this would make me more or less popular within the group, I knew it needed to be said and he, I hope, would understand his role if I were to speak up. The only issue is I must also respect my elders, so I can't necessarily say I thought it would go down well.

'Yes Niyah.' He responded.

'Please understand what I am going to say is not to disrespect you, but to explain what has happened over the years and why it's caused the rift between us.' I swallowed hard as the words left my lips. An earthquake shook my body and I trembled like a leaf.

When raised to respect your elders and with such love poured into me as a child, reminding me of my worth, it was difficult to speak out to my grandparents. With all eyes on me from my cousins who I knew didn't like me, I feared that it would also backfire from them.

'I think I understand why both yourself and Mama would constantly tell me I was the one, or that the hand of God was upon me, or that the ancestors rejoiced at my birth.' I began, 'But in the eyes of others, it seemed as though you placed me on a higher pedestal.'

'I'm not sure if any of my cousins have an African middle name. But I know my siblings do not, so that leaves me under the impression that this is the reason you have said these things.'

His eyes were saddened. Hands beginning to clench. Jaw tightened. He was not happy with what I was saying but I carried on.

'As beautiful as they are, as thoughtful as they are, to those around, it leaves me as the black sheep. There was a lot of attention given to me from both of you,but to my aunts and uncles it would have seemed as though you didn't love their children as much as you did me.'

I heard low murmurs of agreement coming from around the room. Though in agreement, there was still bitterness in their tone.

My grandparents looked disappointed, but I couldn't sit back to see the same thing happening in my family that I tried to help my families to fight through when I was at work. As it was getting late, and with all I had said, my grandmother asked for some help in the kitchen to serve dinner. You may have guessed, her upset at my words meant I was not asked into the kitchen, nor was my presence acknowledged when I went in.

Had these kinks been ironed out much earlier on, it would not have gotten to this. My cousins would have been able to get to know me beyond my name. They would have met a fun loving Niyah. I may not have been molested by my cousin. I wouldn't have found it difficult to understand love within the Black home.

I can't allow myself to feel such disappointment

going forward though. If only I had understood life and what it was to mean at the time, I guess I would have been willing to forgive with much more ease then. Now, I understand and I am working on my ability to forgive. I can't tell what it warranted then, but my mindset now has changed. It's different. I am no longer mad at them.

How my family treated me as a child had a lot to do with their mindset, what my parents allowed, what my grandparents said. How they treated me during the end of my teens, early twenties, was more to do with me. I'm ready for change, but I know it will be difficult.

But things happen. Life happens in an unfortunate way and we just need to learn through the pains we have been through. Easier said than done, but healing comes when we've faced the negatives of our past, head on.

You know what I'm going to say now don't you? That's it for today. I'm going to try to clear my head and cleanse for today. Start the week afresh.

With a new found purpose, I am signing that my crown IS cherished.

Niyah Adenike Thomas.

Monday 18h August 2019
Time: 11:47am

Dear Orion,

Is it too early for this? Have I grown a little too comfortable taking you all around with me? Do I have a problem?

I MANIFESTED KYRON! I am in disbelief!

He text me about an hour ago, but as I was with a client, I wasn't able to text back at the time.

This is really just a quick entry to say that to you. I couldn't contain my excitement and thought it would be weird. Well, it's not weird, but I didn't want to text that to the girls.

I'll catch up with you later though. I saw my client who inspired me to stop wearing my weaves, so I want to fill you in on that.

For now, I will end with kisses.

N.A.T.

Monday 18th August 2019
Time: 8:44pm

Dear Orion,

    I had wished to sit under candle light on many nights to embrace its glow in hopes it would explain to me what I hated. Tonight, I sit under the moon light with candle lights dancing, entertaining stars as I allow my hatred to reverberate in the vacuous hole I have created within me.
    Today was another one of those days I wish had not happened. So yes, we started with that text from Kyron, which made me excited beyond belief. You know this because I came and told you. But after Kyron was the death of me. After Kyron came the unfortunate. The unfortunate disbelief. My past before my future.
    I really wanted to tell you about the Queen I spoke with today, but to have that flashback to my past, I wasn't ready.
    Ricardo. Ricardo popped up. He was one of my clients. I wish I would have been warned. I wish I would have been told prior to walking into the meeting room. And to top it off, my line manager decided it was a good idea for me to take his case, even though he is my family member.
    It would make much sense if I were able to decline the case. Keep his story personal aside. Give him the privacy he would need from me, his cousin.
    He enjoyed my discomfort. He could see it in my body language as I was unable to hide it. When I saw him at my grandparent's house, I could cope. Seeing him alone at work, having a meeting with me, about the issues he is facing in his relationship, felt unprofessional to me.
    I would have loved to tell him that his issues, his sickness, caused me to be ill over the years. I wanted to tell

him that I had lost a child, after becoming promiscuous, having attempted suicide.

It's difficult to do that when you are at work. When you are the one who takes the case, it's not possible to come clean in that way.

I was to be the one who was in charge. The one who was to be in control. I was to let him tell his story and break down. Instead, I absorbed his story and allowed it to take over my emotions.

At the end of the meeting I was ready to file a complaint against my manager, however, I had no good grounds to do that. No-one knew I was holding on to childhood traumas brought on by Ricardo, thus, to put in a complaint to say my manager didn't put my wellbeing before the job, would be void.

'Niyah, I'm happy to have you instead of anyone else.' He had said. 'Can you imagine me telling a stranger my business? At least you know the truth about me so I won't even have to tell you everything.'

He wanted to be silent about his truth whilst I squirmed in my seat knowing he was the root of my sexual frustrations.

'Honestly cuz, I'm scared. I'm in a relationship with a single mother, I can get sex whenever I'm ready, but, you know –' He paused as he searched my eyes as though waiting for me to say it. 'Avery.'

Trying to maintain my composure, I replied, 'Ricardo, in order for me to be of any help to you, I am going to need you to say what's on your mind. I'm not trying to rush your process of opening up, but I can only help you based on what you say.'

I explained that I needed to make notes of what was said in our meeting and with that I knew he would remain silent about Avery as that would surely raise alarm bells. Our confidentiality procedure was quite simple; they say whatever they want to us and we keep quiet unless we believe they are a danger to themselves or to someone else. In this case, Avery would be in danger. He was silent.

I would have loved to be open and honest about his ways, but stuck between the brewing family conflict and the association I would have to a paedophile, whilst trying to keep my job, I'd be given the sack in an instant. They would not be able to trust me knowing that I have kept the identity of a paedophile a secret.

It's the secret which is the problem for me. This secret is toxic. His secret is toxic. How can a man be comfortable with what he has done? Is he even here to get help or just to hope that someone will be able to give him the thumbs up?

'Niyah I just need someone to talk to man. This woman wants me to connect with her children, but I can't. She has two daughters and a son, but how do I tell this woman that I can't trust myself around her daughters, ever.

'You would need to see a counsellor and someone to help you further. I can refer you if you wish.' I said blandly.

I feared that this would end my job had I carried on with him. If he stayed within our service, I didn't see that ending very well for me either. I needed to get him out. Pass him on to someone else. Better yet, force him to seek help on his own. That way, there would be no connection between us and my job would be safe.

Had I been able to see the future, I would have turned him in the instant the situation came to light about him and Avery. I would have turned him in the day I realised how detrimental his freedom would have been to my present, and possibly future too.

'It's cool Niyah. You don't wanna help your own cousin. I see that. What about that big talk you put down when we went to Mama dem house?' He poured his venom in my eyes, piercing my soul with his sharp gaze. 'You were the one talking about taking on the blame. How about now? Is you pawning me off on someone else to help me? Or is it that you're so ashamed of me, you don't want anyone knowing? They see all your notes right? Put that in your notes Niyah!' He spat. 'Tell them I raped you! Tell them you don't trust me. Tell them I've become the black sheep of the family. Tell them that you are in here pissing yourself because I'm sure you've been having flashbacks since I've been here.'

He was right, but I couldn't tell him that. I couldn't tell him that it was the truth. To be honest with him was to have him win. This wasn't something for him to win at. But he does need help.

But why me Orion? Why was I the one he saw? I'm sure the universe was against me.

N.A.T

I'm over and done with the drama my trauma
wants to bring,
The forefather of my today.
The harsh reality I have faced,
The winded feelings I have felt.

I'm over and done with the tasted disgust I've felt,
The arcade of emotions,
The jazz splits of torment,
The spent expeditions of everyone else's want-
ing.

I am just that, just that bitch ready to kill,
Ready for the kill,
Ready for the death of the deaths,
For the death of him.

Ready to push through the pisses of being
pissed on and pissed off,
And no deep breaths can take,
No deep breaths can eradicate,
No deep breath can make me feel better.

I've meditated and manifested
His throat split,
His piss point cut,
His body ache at all joints,
For I've joined in with being bitter,
And there is nothing sweet about it.

I'm over and done with the surprises life throws
at me
For each day has birthed a new emotion
New formula

Love in Black

Clocks are the hands of life always reminding us
To be constant is to be present
And to be present is to be aware,
Aware of the precipice we stand upon
When faced with our darkest fears
And possible regrets.

Tonight, I've lost. I'm losing sleep as I watch
Darkness in its growth
Hoping I'd not be burdened with the birth cere-
mony of dawn.

Dawn, she would have been my hope for better
days.
I wished for a girl before I took matters into my
hands.
Bloody.
I know I've committed murder,
No surprise.

We, I am greater than my pressured thoughts
Once I'm able to give into the lies I sell to myself

<u>Tuesday 19th August 2019</u>
<u>Time: 1:50am</u>

Hey ma,
It's good to see you.
Haven't managed to catch up with you.
I guess you've moved on
Legs wide
Still
Allowing truckers to drive through.

How old would I be today?
Do you think of me?
Actually, I know the answer
I've frequented your thoughts on occasions
You were never able to physically bury me
Your womb now my tomb
Memories of me you cut
Will always be unearthed.

Love in Black

Tuesday 19th August 2019
Time: 2:27am

I

CAN'T

SLEEP!

Tuesday 19th August 2019
Time: 3:05am

This is how it went.

Me: Hey, you up?

Kyron: Yeah, you good?

Me: Nope. I'm frustrated.

Kyron: *wink*

Me: Wanna come round?

Kyron: I'm there.

So now, I'm waiting for Kyron to come round. I know it's not right, but honestly, this is the only way I can cope. I have had a glass of wine, just to prepare my mind for what's about to happen. I'm nervous. We've done this before, but it doesn't stop me getting nervous.

I've freshened up, shaved and oiled myself down.

He should be here soon.

Dear Orion,

He was everything my body ordered. His lips journeyed my body as though they were on an adventure seeking treasure.

It was a passionate lust-filled escapade.

Drunk sex does not compare to what happened and I have had my fair share of those encounters.

The minute I opened the door I saw the thirst in his eyes. My heart exploded. Love, I knew, would have no place here with us.

He pulled me into him in one swift motion. That's when I knew there was no going back.

I was lost in a haze of him. High off the way my body felt in his presence. The ecstasy which surrounded us elevated my need for him.

One minute we were tongue deep in each other's mouths. The next, my legs were wrapped around him, top off, his face in my chest. My heartbeat pulsates between my legs. My head flew back as he gave my breasts the attention they craved. Tongue moving professionally across both. Neither left unattended for too long.

My body writhed under his hot breath. An uncharted calling.

It felt good to be back in his arms. To be in a place of unjudged, consensual bliss led me to making joyful noises. I sang in his favourite pitch of falsetto yet not falsifying my satisfaction, my tunes well versed in the motion of his strokes.

I can't tell how it happened, but I found myself to be on my back in the middle on the sofa with my legs wrapped around him, biting down on his collarbone, nails deep in his back,

His hands took no caution as he explored me; I submitted to their guidance. One hand around my throat, the other holding my hands above my head. Hips bucking in sync. My moans were his GPS. We rode waves together. Orion, I can't tell you how much I have missed him. His lips. His kiss. The blessing between my thighs.

There is so much more I'm withholding from you, but, I think one day this will be found by one of my future children, and I can't have them thinking too many wrongs about their mother.

Thus, for now, I'll leave this where it is.

Love,

N.A.T

Dear Orion,

After last night, I could not stop thinking about Kyron. I fought the thoughts of him during my meetings, yet I still lost. More than once, I lost track of what my clients were saying as his body trod across my mind.

I had wanted to put him behind, but instead, I ended up underneath and on top of him.

I need to be honest about my promises to myself though. I can't allow myself to wind up in another of those situations again. I can't keep going back to Ky because my body misses him, or because I'm down in the dumps and need a release. If I allow for this to continue it will only be a recipe for disaster.

I can't keep using him as a tool for recovery. I want to be loved. I want to be more than just a craving.

I've got a bad case of wanting to be desired and needing to understand how to be loved. I want to be more than a lady who helps families to love each other. I want to be the lady with her own family, learning how to love and cherish each other.

I can hear Ayomide screaming at me as I write this. I don't know if I can tell her about the pleasure I received without her crucifying me.

If I were to be asked how I allowed myself to be drawn in once again, I would have to be truthful that I am the one who drew the cards this time around. All he did was say yes and agreed to coming over.

Today was difficult. If I were to try to have this conversation with anyone close to me, they would either make Ky out to be a sex craved individual or make me out to be a slut. More likely, the latter.

No-one would care for the fact that I was in a bad place and had no mind for a healthy way to handle my situation. They would definitely call me careless. To some, promiscuity to deal with sexual traumas doesn't add up. It still doesn't add up to me even, but being sex drunk takes all pains away.

Anyway, I'm off tomorrow, so I will use tonight as my wash night. I need something else to occupy my thoughts right now.

With a new found purpose, I'm signing my crown is cherished.

Love,

Niyah Adenike Thomas

Dear Orion,

I am more beneficial to others than I am to myself. I can give a world of advice to others, but nothing I've said to them really holds for me.

I am quick to tell families to learn to forgive themselves as individuals yet I still haven't forgiven myself for the things I've done as a child and a teen. Hell, with recent events, I had not, before now, considered forgiving myself.

We do tend to forget to forgive ourselves at times; we forget that we are deserving of forgiveness. We do not always make the right decisions and then beat ourselves up afterwards. The difficulty I believe, in forgiving one's self is that we've never been taught how to. We've not been taught the importance of forgiving ourselves in comparison to the importance paid to forgive others. In all honesty, I don't think we know how to forgive anyone. It is something thrown around and I feel the attachment to religion holds selfishness in it. To be specific, Christianity.

In church we are told to forgive others, that Our Father in Heaven will forgive us. That being the case, it means, I should not forgive you out of love for you, but for the want to be seen as closer to God. When you do this, you have a better shot at getting into the Kingdom.

It has barely made sense to me. Why is it that whether I'm forgiven for my wrong doings come from an ultimatum? No-one has ever told me that it was important for me to look into my actions, those carried out from learnt behaviours, to understand why I did what I did and why I need to forgive myself for them.

Saying that, it is something I have learned over the

years though I've not been adhering to self-forgiveness as I should. I am aware that my controversial views would lead to the brewing of arguments from deeply entrenched Christians. But, I can't remember forgiveness being linked to love. Love has always been the distant cousin of Forgiveness whom you rarely hear about. If the two aren't seen as a remedy for healing, how can we expect anything?

Also, have our Black Pastors been misled by those who taught them? Has our past really taught us nothing about being able to redeem ourselves from our mistakes? Is it that we've subconsciously learnt that we aren't deserving of pardon?

I just want to understand the underlying factors to be honest, Orion.

Why were we never taught to forgive ourselves? Is it because we've always seen each other being put away for small crimes, even when innocent, thus teaching us we aren't worthy of second chances? Is there a way to reprogramme the way we view ourselves and our worth?

I do wonder how much influence slavery has on us. I can't help but think this interruption to our history has etched a deep sense of falsehood in us which has pulled its way into our today. Unfortunately, it will also drive itself into our future.

I do want to veer off from this thought, move it into a different direction, but, I just don't know how to. I guess I'll come back to it later on. <u>SLAVERY DID NOT AFFECT AMERICANS ALONE</u>

They've said to hide things from Blacks
They should put it into books.
In their minds we lack intelligence;
Brains unformed, they treat us like animals,
Yet taught us their religion
All the while brainwashing us further.

The Bible to be our salvation.
The Bible to restore our hope,
That which they stole from us.
The Bible to give us our purpose.
The Bible to teach us our identity.

We with guilt,
We're born into sin.
Forced to till a land which was never our own
Taught to obey our masters.
They then became our creators
Creating all forms of necessary evil.

Forgive them seventy times seven.
Forgive them never meant us being forgiven by
them
But by the Heavenly Father.

It's no wonder we struggle today.
We ask God for forgiveness
And man looks at us with a gut heavy with laughter.

On numerous occasions, I have had to tell my families that they ought not keep themselves tied to the mistakes they have made. Some of the things we do are from traumas we have faced. Even out of love, parents are at times unaware of what it is they are doing, that the discipline they are giving is mostly linked to how they themselves were raised and the unresolved problems they have faced.

Though I say we, I think I ought to be more specific and be more honest with myself. This is more about me than others and if I continue to see this as a community issue, it will only leave me naïve and in a position where I continue to lie to myself.

From this point on, I'll work on forgiving myself.

If I can forgive myself first, I do not need to worry about whether I'll be forgiven by others. I need to be able to hold myself accountable so I can work towards becoming a better version of me, daily.

It works with the idea of not seeking validation from others. If I value myself and can disprove of my own behaviours, I can also approve of the good I do. I can love myself for what I have to offer to myself instead of waiting for someone to come in and do that before I'm able to.

Where do I even begin?

I have childhood traumas. Teenage years of questioning my worth. A near death experience brought on by myself. Sexual promiscuity. Family disliking me due to misunderstandings and possible jealousy.

I've got a lot of untangling to do before I'm able to properly move forward.

I may need a huge sheet of paper to map out where to begin and how to begin. But not tonight.

Bye Orion.

N.A.T

Love in Black

It's puzzling

Friday 22nd August 2019

Dear Orion,

   What does one do when they have changed their dependencies? When they have stopped focussing on the relationships they had previously used to save them? What should they do? How do they continue their new normal when their old reality pops up?
   As a Black Woman, the expectations are high. I should be loving. I must maintain my composure at all times if I do not want to fall into the stereotype of being an Angry Black Woman, or as I put it, an ABW. I must protect my Black Men. If I had a family, I would need to keep my house functioning; be the referee when my children fight. Be the chef, decorator, and everything else. When it comes to friends, I need to be their confidant. I must forgive them. I must put their wellbeing before mine.
   What about the expectations to put myself first you ask? That doesn't exist in this world. It's not yet normalcy. Will it ever be? I would hope so, but, for now, it sucks!
   With there being so many unhealthy expectations, it's easy for us to self-sabotage. We, as women, do not know how to put ourselves first as it was never taught to us. Something I wish to work on for the sake of my own sanity. It's the reason I started meditating; I needed to focus on me above the needs of others.
   I do have to truly thank Ayomide for the introduction to the practice. Funny enough, in church they used to talk about meditating on the Words of God but it didn't sink in. I had no clue as to what I was to do. Now, now I set aside the time to breathe, focus on me, ponder on my affirmations.
   As good as it all sounds though, I am unable to stick to the routine. This is what I meant about not knowing how

to forgive myself. I have been so hard on myself in the past because I've not managed to go more than a month with my meditation practice.

I can only say that goes back to my childhood. We were not allowed to 'give up' because then we'd be called failures. We couldn't decide that we wanted to simply take a break, that was too similar to 'giving up'.

I know I've seen this in movies; Black families treat each other as toxins if they 'quit'. I do not, however, remember seeing that with many White families on my screen.

Was this something taught? Is this something our parents learned from their parents, who got that from their ancestors? Yes, I'm going to ask it. Is this something we picked up from slavery which has become a part of us? Slave masters abusing our families if they stopped working, is this what has caused us to be brainwashed?

We must find a way to move forward to allow ourselves to be better without feeling ashamed of wanting to do something different.

I'll not be that parent to my children. I need them to freely move between activities to find what they love. What use is it being trapped within one role and not knowing what more is out there for you?

To a degree, I can say I understand a certain celeb couple and the way they raise their children. By giving them space to roam, they have had the opportunity to experiment in life. I'd adopt a similar principle with my children. Follow their lead, see where their interest lies, arrange for them to take part in related activities. If it's something I'd need to pay membership for, I feel I would go for a monthly contract, just in the event they no longer want to do it after two months or so, I can cancel the subscription without paying a leaving fee.

Even with all that, I would ensure I teach them about

enduring the things they dislike, but would not be able to up and leave. Biggest example, school.

You can't just change courses because you have no interest in it, and it doesn't mean you shouldn't strive to excel in that class. This is a mindset which many of us do not have. Admittedly it's one which I too held, but I'd say now I know better.

As Blacks, we need to make room for changing activities without being shamed for it. We need to allow our children to feel comfortable to find their way and leave activities they feel aren't for them. We must support and trust that their souls know what's best and what's not working for them.

That's it from me for today though.

With the purpose I have and the knowledge I own that my crown is cherished, I will say goodbye.

Love,

Niyah Adenike Thomas.

Your worth isn't set by your bank account
He has no right to use finances to define you

Date: Saturday 23rd August 2019
Time: 7:00pm

Dear Orion,

I've just had to cancel a date. The guy I was to meet had all the right words until he told me that I would have needed to bring proof of my finances with me to our date.

He was cute, but honestly, looks can't save anyone when it comes to trust. For you to project your trust issues onto me so early, when we aren't even dating. That's problematic.

His demand felt extremely intrusive and it reminded me of one of my clients. She was married to a man who was financially controlling her for years. In our fourth session, she came to see me in floods of tears.

Her divorce had been finalised and she barely got anything from it. Everything was in his name, and, to top it off, she had signed a prenup.

In their prenuptial agreement, it was stated that if they were to divorce, she couldn't go after anything in his name. She mentioned, in between sobs, that she had not given it a second thought at the time as they were renting a flat together when they had just gotten married; at that point, both their names were on the lease.

She had not realised that saving up half of the deposit for their mortgage didn't mean her name would be on the mortgage. Had she not been burnt out from home-schooling their first child and being pregnant with their second, she would have been more aware of what had been going on in her marriage. With everything and her mind being elsewhere, it was easy for him to put his name as sole owner, which left her and the children as lodgers.

When it came to her getting a job, he insisted she took something part-time so they wouldn't need to hire a babysitter, nor would they need to leave the children with childminders as they got older.

Our meeting consisted of tears streaming down her face as I handed her boxes of tissues.

With my meeting as a memory, I didn't want to enter into something which would leave me distraught. Thus, this guy, this man child, who wanted proof of my finances, definitely had to be dropped off my list in an instant.

I still can't get over the fact he was so bold and brazen with it. He said it with his whole chest. The audacity. As my mother would say, him bright and facety. I was not the least bit impressed, but am happy we got that out of the way early.

Can you imagine he hadn't asked and we went on several dates, then one night he and I got to drinking, which did not lead to sex but instead, it would have led to us talking about finances and him 'comparing' our expenditures and credit scores. An intoxicated me would have entertained his nonsense.

Unfortunately, for some women, those pressured by their families to get married, they would have been caught. It could go one of two ways, either he ditches them because it's not high enough, or keeps them because he believes a woman with a low score would be easily manipulated.

The thought of it makes me feel really uncomfortable. What is it which leaves a man making moves like this?

I am very proud of myself. I am proud of not having sabotaged myself. I didn't talk myself into going on that date, nor did I seek validation based on my finances.

I'm going to take the rest of tonight to just chill. I might dance around for a bit, sing some songs, but I will not wallow. I will continue to swipe through the plethora of men in my palms. I'm quite certain I'll meet someone worthy.

I hope.

It's always scary going on these dates, not knowing the person on the other end. Do they really look like their photos? Are they as emotionally intelligent as they come off?

Thoughts such as these have made me hesitant about online dating, but I've got to put myself out there somehow seeing as I am more of a homebody.

This is why Kyron was such an easy option. He is someone I know and trust. There is no pressure there. The downside is that he is emotionally unavailable, this I'd known before getting involved. It would be careless of me to go any further.

Anyway, you know what time It is.

We'll catch up tomorrow. Whilst writing, I've been texting another guy. Tell you more tomorrow.

N.A.T

Date: Sunday 24th August 2019
Time: 7:27am

Dear Orion,

Time to fill you in! This guy's name is David. He is cute! Very easy on the eyes! Very easy. At this point I feel shallow, but it's what his photos give me.

I like our conversations. They flow well. He's like a refreshing jug of lemonade. We've also spoken on the phone, effortlessly. He's definitely one I've put in the running, one I'd love to go on a date with.

These are the things I know about him thus far:

1) He is Jamaican (double points)

2) He has a job with the NHS and has been working for them for the past four years (doubly double points)

3) He has a child but hasn't seen him in a while (not sure how I feel about this. Maybe half point? Zero? Minus point?)

4) He likes animals (one point)

5) He doesn't live far from my parents (scary but maybe one point)

6) He wants to go on a date pretty soon (ONE HUNDRED POINTS!)

I don't think we are rushing. I feel this is right. When we meet, we'll be able to feel the vibe between us. Our souls will determine whether we will speak or meet again.

I have a beautiful view and it's been giving me a blessing. I want to use this sunrise as a reason I should go ahead with this date. I woke up at 4:30am, to start my day off with yoga. Yoga followed by hues of red, orange and pink taking over the sky. It was the sultry dress the sky wore to my ball telling me yes, go on that date.

How today will end, I'm not particularly sure, but I'm hopeful. I figure things will go according to a higher plan.

My thing about this all is that I question whether it's right for me to try to take my love's fate into my own hands. I want to love, I want to be loved, but I can't help but feel that this is wrong. Nevertheless, I'll still go on these dates, despite my initial reservations.

* * *

'Would you ever do online dating?' Ayomide asked as we looked at online ads about finding the perfect match.

'Not unless I was beyond desperate' I laughed.

One of our friends had been studying Psychology and told us about an assignment which intrigued us. Tonight, we decided to drink a little and were under the influence to go digging.

'Why are there so many old men on this?'

'Maybe because Jane is a 40 year old woman.' I blurted. Ayomide lost control of the chuckle she was trying to stifle.

'Why did we create a profile for a 40 year old woman?' I had no answer for her.

As we continued on our drunken search for no-one in particular, we noticed some of the advances being made on this woman, this Jane who we created were border-line psychotic and full blown pervy.

'Ayomide,' I began, 'if I ever decide to do any form of online dating, please kill me.'

'Never!'

'What? Why not?'

'I will need to vicariously live through you.'

'No! This is insane. Look at what these men are saying!'

* * *

I was nineteen when I told Ayomide to keep me away from online dating. I guess I was desperate to have now ventured to the dark side.

I'll give Ayomide a call later on. It has been some time

since she and I spoke. To have been so close, she was my best friend and possibly still is, it's a shame this is what has caused me to think about her.

At the age of nineteen, neither of us knew online dating would become such a big thing. The new way to date. Neither of us realised this was not just for over forties, but also reached out to those in their twenties as well.

It's also that thing women do when they feel as though their clock is ticking. Well, that's what happens in the movies. I guess that's how I felt when I signed up. That, and knowing I go from home to work and back again without much else excitement.

It has also been a while since being out with the girls, but I don't believe I'd meet someone on a night out. Well, I could, but to meet a guy at a club or bar sounds irresponsible to me.

Is it more irresponsible to get to know someone I've met at a bar than it is to meet someone from a dating app?

I believe I will go ahead with this date.
For now, I'll go enjoy today.
N.A.T

Knowing your worth
Is the only key you need
Your value never depletes
Despite your insecurities
Let no-one allow you
To think otherwise.

<u>Date: Wednesday 27th August 2019</u>

Dear Orion,

My spirit and human nature were at war. Feelings of inadequacy had set in and it hurt. Why did he not call or text me? What was it that allowed him to feel I was no longer good enough for him to meet?

This is the first time I've ever been stood up, so all possible questions popped up.

I left work in good time to allow myself to get home, have a shower, do my hair and makeup as well as including time to try on at least 3 outfits. I cannot believe I got ready and waited for hours, hoping he would call, or text. I got nothing.

For the past couple of days I've been wallowing in self-pity and found it difficult to concentrate. It wasn't until speaking with a client today I was able to understand the true meaning of self-worth. The last time I came to you, I did come across as though I knew and understood what self-worth meant, however, this situation showed me that I didn't. My client today inadvertently helped me.

What has amazed me most of all today is that it doesn't matter that I've been working in this field for several years, I keep learning what some may call 'simple' lessons from my clients. I'm always grateful for lessons.

I won't really go into it all when it comes to this guy, but I was foolish to believe that things could progress with him. I barely knew him yet trusted him. Right now, I want to get myself some rest.

By continuing to think about him, I will pull myself back into a bad place. That, my friend, will be it for now.

N.A.T

My peace of mind is as still as the moon's glow.
She is untampered with when night draws on
her
And during the sun's brawl, she rages when
stared upon.
Do not challenge her to a duel,
It's never something she wishes to get into
But with forced hands, she calmly unleashes
uncomfortable truths.
Your lips become sealed,
Hearts will run ragged,
Your days will seem numbered.

But she is untamed,
Not yet taught how to waltz in rooms of unfa-
miliarity.
She despises the battle she faces with worth,
Learning its purpose amongst her.
She finds her feet to be heavy
As she trudges through the unknown.
My peace of mind lacks her time with peace.
She wants what she needs but fails to go after
it,
So I'm gifting her with patience
Allowing her to move at her own pace.

<u>Date: Thursday 30th August 2019</u>

Dear Orion,

Today, my thoughts danced around my not so virgin womb and the child I could eventually carry. To be specific, the son I could introduce to this world.

Here in the UK, little Black boys are lost to gangs, stolen by groomers. In America, little Black boys, Black teenage males, and Black men are stolen by bullets belonging to those who are meant to protect. This is only the tip of an iceberg which exists. This is not short of being terrifying. It shook me to the core.

Can you therefore be upset with any Black woman or Black man who wants to have an interracial relationship? They can only hope that their son, by being of a fairer complexion, would be saved from this somehow. We could argue that those who wish to get into interracial relationships just to have a mixed raced child do not know their worth. However, it's a lot more than knowing your worth.

Imagine knowing your worth yet feeling trapped. No matter how much you try to live up to it, you are pulled down. Would you want your child to experience the same thing? You've not yet found a way out, you're managing to barely cope, still learning about how to navigate through all the turmoil life throws at you, your back is against the wall.

Would you want the children you are to bring into the world to face the hardships you've faced?

Please understand, I'm not saying it's the right mentality to have. What I am saying is that I understand. It makes sense as to why some Blacks would seek relationships with those outside the race so their offspring would be of mixed heritage.

As for me, there are enough lessons I've learnt which I can pass on. However, how do I protect my son? I can constantly remind him of how loved he is. I can hope that his father and I maintain our relationship so he has a nuclear home to return to every day. I can kiss and hug him from birth. I can teach him about his importance, and give tools to remind him of these. But, I can't always be by his side, at school, or on the road. If we were to move to America, my being next to him in a car may not stop a police officer from shooting him.

I'll not be getting in a relationship with a White man, or an Asian, my son to be mixed. With his father, we will all navigate through this cold world, Black.

I do fear my lessons will not be good enough for him.

I guess I'd write letters to him, daily reminders of my love for him. I hope my love will be enough to keep him going down the wrong path.

How do single mothers do it? How do they give their sons guidance and love and teach them to be men? How do they ensure these boys do not become drug dealers, caught in the middle of gang cultures, and stay out of prison?

How do nuclear families do it? How did my parents do it? Do they tag team when it comes to parenting? Does the father have sit down sessions with his son to discuss life through the eyes of a Black man? Did my father do this?

All of this stemmed from looking at a family that came into the office today. They weren't on my caseload, but I did overhear two of my colleagues talking about them. Stacey and Naomi. They were in the kitchen standing by the kettle making their midday coffee. The family were on Naomi's caseload; I've always thought her to be very good at her job, until this moment.

'I just don't get why they have the nerve to blame the

system,' Naomi had told Stacey as she interlaced her fingers around her mug.

'They have been parents for thirteen years, so you would have thought they would be able to reign their child in.' She had continued while staring into the depths of the black ocean in her hand. I wonder if she stared as deeply into the pupils of her clients. I wonder if her staring into the coffee reminded her of staring into the eyes of her clients. The killer sentence is what followed Orion. This so and so of a woman had the nerve to say 'Black people are always blaming the system' as she glanced over at me. It's as though she said that in hopes I would jump in. If that were the case, her wish was my command. I did.

I stood up, gathered my items as an air of uncertainty lingered. I looked over at them both, my face with extreme dissatisfaction, 'maybe we would stop blaming the system if we could trust that those who are there to support and help, would do so with an honest heart.'

With that, I left. I do not know anything about that family's case, but I do know that their caseworker would not have their best interests at heart. That being said, I can safely say it's not the system which fails. It feels like the system because to keep hitting brick walls after different individuals are put in place to help, yet you are still left in the cold, it feels as though everyone is against you.

I think I'll leave it here today Orion. The thought of it all is depressing me, and I can only pray to God that my son will be well. I do hope that he will be covered and not harmed by evil adversaries.

Orion, with the purpose I do remember, I'm signing that my crown is cherished.

Niyah Adenike Thomas.

I can't exchange partitions and introductions
So, instead, I'll teach.
I can't exchange mistreatments or misunder-
standings
So, instead, I'll pray.
I can't exchange you for anyone else
And I never would
So, instead I'll love.

I will love you with all my might,
I won't swaddle, but I will hang on to you for as
long as I can
Because, honestly, I fear you'll be taken without
permission,
I fear you will be stolen from me
And our borrowed time will become memories.
Similar to me memorising this piece
And being stuck in this loop
Hoping I -
Similar to me memorising this piece
And being stuck in this loop
Hoping I -
Similar to me memorising this piece
And being stuck in this loop
Hoping I remember each point.
Each tip of the iceberg which has toppled me
over,
My emotions being spun like a top

I must remember why I fight
And why my cheeks will be tear stained upon
knowing
That you will have taken residence in my what
once was virgin womb
Which now feels similar to a tomb because son,

I am afraid that you will be taken too soon
And your dreams would have only been safer if
you had not been brought forth,
If the sun had never kissed your Black skin,
If you would never have gone from Prince to
King.

Son, I am afraid that your skin will have been tat-
tooed with targets invisible to your eyes,
But to predators, you would be marked,
Your every move under the radar
And no matter how careful you are,
They would find you
Take you under their wings,
Teach you how to be stealthy so you'd hide your
new way of being from your father and I

I can only pray that we teach you with love,
That our lessons to you will not go unheard,
That you will take heed to our warnings and that
Good God Almighty will not forsake you.
I hope, that you will not crave acceptance from
anyone,
That your worth will be so well known by you
You will not lower your standards to fit in and
will be comfortable standing out,
That your strength be in your aura and you will
be no-one's prey.

I pray, my son, that you will be okay
But I cannot promise that I will one day stop
worrying about you.
I know I won't be able to always protect you,
That one day you will kiss my cheek and tell me
you'll be just fine,

Tell me not to worry and you will be home late
But, I, like my parents, will sit up with worry
dripping in my veins.
My nerves unsettled.
I will remember that this world isn't safe
And the night is the devil's playground
So anything will be possible
And there is a possibility that the dart will find
you as the bullseye they have been seeking
And poison will reign in your veins
And my son will no longer be recognisable to
me.

My fears are walking nightmares which have
taken on the form of people
Whose aim is to kill love,
Steal light,
And destroy foundation,
That they may be the new place of hope to
those they have broken

My Prince, I hope my love is enough to sustain
you.
I hope your father's love is enough to maintain
you.
I hope our lessons are enough to restrain you.

I can't exchange partitions and introductions
So, instead, I'll teach.
I can't exchange mistreatments or misunder-
standings
So, instead, I'll pray.
I can't exchange you for anyone else
And I never would
So, instead I'll love.

Dear Orion,

It's a journey like no other. I've never noticed how important it is and how much work is required, but I hope to continue enjoying myself through each step. It only hit me today that it's more difficult than I initially thought when it comes to unlearning traumas. Something as simple as loving yourself comes with the quest to be able to safely navigate through not only those I have faced as an individual, but also the strains of others I have taken on. These ordeals were not always known to me as they were occurring and some have trickled down through generations.

Fun fact: parents parent the way they were parented. In how many ways can I use the word 'parent' right? All I mean is, what a parent learns whilst they are growing up, they either keep with them or decide against repeating when they themselves have children. If an individual is unable to recognise their personal barriers and traumas as they grow, they will eventually repeat subconsciously.

This is why I have chosen to get to know me better.

I want to be able to give my future children all of the best parts of me without overcompensating or neglecting their needs. I can say the trials I have faced have come to be a driving force in my life and I've never noticed that they began as a child.

I do wonder if my parents were conscious of the fact that they may have been repeating what their parents did as they were growing up.

Now this is where the issue with my name and how I have been treated in my family comes in. My grandparents had no idea that by putting me on a pedestal it would cause rifts within the family. No one likes favour-itism when they are not the one being favoured. When you aren't the one being favoured, you develop a taste of dislike for the one living the high life. It's also possible that the one who is showing the favouritism gets disliked also by extension. This dislike if not addressed then slow-ly morphs into hatred.

Sounds familiar right?

Well, I've learnt from experience that this is not some-thing I'd like to happen with my children, or grandchil-dren, and thus, I won't do it when it's my turn to be the role model.

It's unfair that others must suffer as a result of an in-dividual not dealing with their personal issues first. This is why I want to begin with me.

With working in the field I currently work, I can only say that it opens my eyes daily. No client has ever failed to teach me a new life lesson.

I do wonder if this is why God has chosen that I re-main single until the moment I have learnt enough of the right lessons to have a child. If I look into the mirror, deeply into my eyes, I must be able to see love amongst the darkness which surrounds this world. If not, I won't be able to effectively guide my child with love.

By now you are possibly thinking I have gone crazy. I started off talking about enjoying each step yet all this while, I have been talking about trauma. I just do not be-lieve that I should allow myself to be poisoned as I learn to heal.

A key lesson in life can be taken from the Akan peo-ple of Ghana. They have symbols called Adinkra symbols which all represent something in life, all with meaning and power. The one which resonates most with me is Sankofa.

It's been this thing which has helped me to keep

going daily and sometimes I do forget about it. Those are the points in time I find that I struggle most of all. Today it has returned, and today I remember what it means. Its meaning is simple yet powerful, going back to past lessons, or past knowledge, and taking it into the present so that the progress made will be positive.

I'm confident that by looking at the lessons I can take from past traumas, I will be able to navigate better throughout whatever is thrown at me today and in the future.

My biggest lesson may just come from the horror of having lost my first child. I was young and had not known how important and powerful I was and would be. I failed to see through my situations and had still been living in the shadows of mistakes made by others. Those mistakes essentially became my own. I can't pretend to put the blame on others when I had intentions of killing myself, and harmed a more innocent being in the process.

I still have flashbacks to that day in the bath. I'm not sure I'll ever get over it, but I do know that I regret it and am ready to take forward with me what I can in order to ensure that this curse does not follow any of my children to come.

If life's lies were lilies,
I guess I'd have them loiter longer,
Linger in every corner,
I'd water them so that they'd grow,
Create their jungle in my home,
Let them take over.

Life's lies aren't lilies,
Yet they have hung around
Each with their own trap door.
A Venus flytrap lays amongst them,
Ready to host home for my truths

That the lies will continue to swell,
I guess I've misjudged my judgement.
I believed in the lie that said I overcame,
Instead, I only came with an untrained mind.
Now I must unlearn the wrongs,
Recreate a new training ground,
Let my new lessons become home for bless-
ings,
Believe in powers higher than I,
That I may be mightier than my previous highs.

That's it from me for today.

With purpose, I'm signing that my crown is cherished.

Niyah Adenike Thomas.

Sept. 2019

From: Marcel

Beauty has eyes set on stars as bright as you. My heart misses you and my eyes can't wait to gaze upon you. We have together conquered pains and today I need you. I need to be with you so that we may tackle my new found pain, loneliness. Do you think I could fight it off with you by my side?

<u>Date: Saturday 1st September 2019</u>

Dear Orion,

Marcel is honestly that guy I'd do anything for and anything with. I'm not sure if I love him as just a friend or if I'd want more from our friendship. Nevertheless, I'm always ready to go to the end of the Earth with him on whatever mission he has. I guess it's to do with the fact he sends me beautiful texts.

Today feels different though. I don't believe I can be at his beck and call for another week or so. I wanted to just bask in a self-care Saturday to bring myself back to where I need to be. I don't know what to say in my reply, but I do know I ought to reply soon enough.

I think he would understand my stance as he always roots for my happiness. I'm not entirely sure if he would understand now or later. I don't know if he would see my case as unimportant in comparison to his. Before today, there has never been a moment when I've had to say can we take a rain check, not unless it was raining and we couldn't get past our front doors. Yes, I know, it's England and it forever rains, but that's never stopped us. We have umbrellas for a reason and he has a car, always had since I've known him.

He would understand right?

Life waits for no-one and I'm willing to use this day to reconnect. I would love to spend it with Marcel, but I can't see it in either of our best interests for me to do so. Completing self-care Saturday means my health and sanity comes first, a rare commodity.

What does my partner in crime say?
Another text. How long can I ignore him?
You're not one to sleep late.
Why you ignoring the lonely guy?

I guess I can't ignore him for much longer. Next thing you know, he'll be at the door ringing the doorbell non-stop. I guess a simple text to say *self-care Saturday today, sorry boo* will have to suffice.

Yoga session, meditation, hot bath (hopefully without the flashbacks) and a face mask does sound exceptional to me. This is the kind of day I have been needing but have not completely indulged in for some time now. Again, needed.

Why did you have to choose the day I'm lonely for self-care? Thought you were to be my partner in crime?

This guy isn't willing to give up is he? I love Marcel, but I'm not able to give into the guilt trip today.

I am your partner in crime, but honestly, I need this time for me today. I need to do some self-work. I need to be alone to be able to reconnect with me.

You've been watching those TEDx videos again haven't you?

He does have an idea of who I am. I'd usually watch the TEDx videos, but this time around it's more to do with seeing the Sankofa symbol which has sparked this.

Love begins with self and today I begin self love. True love. I want to be able to offer love to a man who is deserving. I need to know what love is to give to my future children. I refuse to issue my children with the pains which have clothed me throughout my life. My husband will not see me as a broken woman.

I suppose this is test one, to see how much I want it. It would not be a worthy task if I were able to get through without any hiccups now would it?

He will have to wait. I can't be sucked into texting him today. That would take away my time which is to be used with myself.

Here we begin with me writing affirmations. From this point forward, I vow to write three affirmations before offloading. I vow to better my outlook on my life and society. I vow to improve my version of self above all else.

The affirmations I write will be what they are for others; positive statements to aid in combating self-sabotage and overcoming negative thoughts.

This is a practice I wish to continue throughout my life and bring into the lives of my children. I want to teach them how to protect their mental health from a young age. I do not want for them to feel as though they are unable to work with their emotions effectively.

I was never taught how to build myself up as a child. I was always saved by my parents, time and time again. Don't get me wrong, I do understand that parents are to be the ones who protect their children, however, that does not mean they should disable their power to heal internally. The misconception which ought to be nullified is that self-healing does not require help from without.

What I mean is that we need to stop failing ourselves, believing that we can work on our turmoil without seeking help from others. True strength is knowing when to ask for help. True strength is pulling the light within to a place where it shines brightly for self as well as others. True strength is withdrawing from situations which expect too much from us.

I want my children to have a coping mechanism in place and to know that their father and I will be there for them whenever they need the support. I'll come back to this tomorrow though. I do need to unravel myself from this book to get my thoughts and heart rate in order.

Before I go, here are three affirmations for today:
1 – My thoughts will become my reality
2 – I am a wonderful sister

3 – I am worthy of love
And with purpose I am signing that my crown is cherished.
Niyah Adenike Thomas

<u>**Date: Sunday 2nd September 2019**</u>

Affirmations:
1 – My will is unstoppable
2 – I only control my reactions, not their actions
3 – I am worthy of love

Dear Orion,

Yesterday was beautiful. Not only did I feel better about myself after writing my affirmations, but I had more energy.

The yoga opened my body up, elongating my spine and allowing my shoulders to drop. The meditation cleared some of the dark fog which had surrounded my mind. The hot bath was the best thing ever. For the perfect bath the recipe is as follows; a lit candle, cherry blossom scent preferably, a few drops of essential oil, and a sakura (cherry blossom) bath bomb.

Sakura is a part of Japanese culture and something I embrace. The flowers represent spring and new beginnings. I am in love with the way the petals fall to the ground during spring. Their beauty is soft and peaceful. As they lay on the ground, they get me thinking about the way in which we, if left untouched, remain perfect and untainted. However, life comes along and puts us through our own hurricanes. The most important thing isn't the petals, it's the trunks and the roots.

Our beauty, our outward appearance is fleeting: the petals. Our mindset, the strength and firmness of our mental health are the roots. No-one is able to see the health of our minds unless it's at a point we can no longer hide, then the roots are unable to pull nutrients from the soil and we are unable to produce within our upcoming spring. We become affected by the weather, stopped from producing, forced hibernation.

Sakura is a reminder of the importance of remaining sturdy in all weathers. Yes, I know I had previously mentioned sakura in relation to friends, but this is different. This is us, individuals, as sakura. This is me as sakura. I need to ensure my roots are deep enough and strong enough to be able to keep my trunk fighting the battles that I will face. To conquer that, I will keep allowing room for new blossoms. I will keep enjoying the time I have here on Earth. I will keep learning, pulling on lessons as my nutrients. I will keep growing.

Now that's out of the way, I've suddenly remembered that I was to continue talking about the affirmations and how I will bring my children up on them. It does link with what I was just saying about Sakura though.

Look at it this way:

The roots seek help from the soil around, stretching deeply below ground. This is how they get their nutrients. I want my children to have their roots deep within myself and their dad, for them to reach out at any point for extra nutrients. The nutrients they receive from us will be from the lessons we have learnt which we can pass on to them. As they grow older, they will find others from whom they can learn. They too will be a source of nutrients for others, but first, they need to be able to learn how to re-energise in such a way which allows for them to not run low, and not give what they do not have.

The trunk is to allow for transport of nutrients from roots to shoots amongst other things. Over time they age and the outer layer of the trunk hardens. My children, their bodies, will be their trunks, the lessons learned will be processed within their mind and how they use it will be down to them. We learn many lessons in life, but the most important thing is what we do with the information we take on board, and whether we take it on in the first place at all.

Now for the blossoms. The weather plays a crucial role in when trees are able to blossom. The weather in this country is quite unpredictable at times. One year spring hits around mid-March, another, it could seemingly come as early as February. Global warming has its way with us. Anyway, the weather my children will come face to face with will determine how well they were able to take heed to the lessons they learnt. There will be some that they have not yet come across, but I would love for them to grab onto those for the next time they need to apply it. They will blossom in and out of season, but I will teach them to keep going no matter what.

That being said, this is why they will learn how and why to write affirmations. I won't wait until they begin to talk to remind them that they are worthy and that they are light. These are words which will be repeated to them continuously so that they will be able to walk in confidence as they say it all.

I will not, however, lead them to believe that everyone they meet will treat them well. They will understand that there will be individuals who will try to speak down to them. As they grow older, they will be able to speak the way they have been taught to speak, with confidence and not arrogance. They will learn how to conduct themselves when someone attempts to belittle them.

If another child is around while I go through affirmations with my children, I will not exclude them from the practice. I do not wish for other children to look upon mine as though they are getting special treatment, though I am their mother. I do not wish that my children be caught up in the same poison I was exposed to as a child. My grandparents had no idea that they were causing me to inherit insecurities from their treatment of me.

Lastly, I will not overcompensate. I cannot overdo and

try to give them all I believe my parents failed at giving me. In addition to that, I will not withhold love from them in fear that I may cause them to feel isolated due to my trying to rectify the wrongs of my grandparents.

I know my children will have their fair share of trials to deal with, thus I do not want to add mine to their list of things to deal with.

I pray they become better at being sustainable beings than I have been. I also pray that whoever is to be their father and my future husband is working on his healing now, so that when we meet, he will have techniques to share with us all.

I guess that's it from me today though Orion.

With purpose I am signing that my crown is cherished.

Niyah Adenike Thomas.

<u>**Date: Monday 3rd September 2019**</u>

Affirmations
1 – I am bigger than my past pains
2 – I will forgive myself for my wrongs
3 – I will not be selfish to myself

Dear Orion,

The day wasn't half bad. I started by finally replying to Marcel, who seemingly made it through the weekend okay without my aid. I am extremely proud of him. I expected that he was going to be very childish about it all and tell me that he'd call me when he was done sulking. I do have to also give myself a pat on the back because I had not been shy about telling him how needed it was on Saturday.

There was also something different about my clients today. They came in, together. I mean, they all, my regular clients, had gone through all the tasks I had previously set them. They, where they were not single parents, had talked things through with each other, so when coming in, they were all on the same page. It was refreshing.

It was refreshing until the end of the day when I had been handed a last minute case, as madame Naomi was sent home due to falling ill after lunch. Conveniently falling ill. The same family she had disrespected in the kitchen was the family she should have been seeing, the ones I was tasked with meeting with.

I'm not mad at the fact that they were handed over to me. I'm just disgusted that she was not able to ask me during the morning when we were both semi-free, not seeing any clients, if I could take over the case. I would have happily said yes and it would have given me the time to read over their case file.

Her incompetence left me stumbling over my words and apologising on her behalf.

The family were happy with my taking on the case, yes, I said taking over the case. As the meeting was about to begin, my wonderful manager, Sandra, came in and introduced me to the family, and the family to me. She then introduced herself before taking my breath with her as she said 'Niyah here, one of our trusted family coach and assistant manager, will be taking the lead on your case and I thought it right to come in and introduce you all.'

The devil in me sat on my shoulder cursing at her. I sat straight, smiled, and observed the family as their bodies lost the rigidity they held. I am happy to know that they were relieved, it meant that the session could continue with no hard feelings. However, this was at 3pm. We had all of today for me to be informed and prepare, yet no-one thought it right to warn me beforehand.

There is really so much surprise my face can take before I crack under reality's heavy hand. Thankfully, meditation is something I had carried on since Saturday and I was playing jazz during the interesting introduction.

Once Sandra had finished her spiel, I was able to speak with the family and get to know them a little better. Seeing as I would be taking on their case, I expressed my apologies for asking them to repeat what it is they would have said in their previous meeting. I wanted to get to know them beyond the notes that were handed over to me. As they were sitting before me, it only made sense that they told me what it was that brought them to seek our services.

Some individuals are referred to us by schools, social services, the youth service, and so forth, others find us by doing searches for themselves online.

This family was referred to us by the school. Their issue stemmed from dad being unable to accept that his son is human and would cry if things got too much for him. He was 13 years old and was having difficulties adjusting to life in a new school. It may be different going forward, but we wouldn't know as he will be returning to school in two days.

I remember hearing about them before. The school was having difficulties with getting in touch with his parents when they tried to make contact and he was always crying in school. School referred them to us before sending the case to social services as they believed that we would possibly be effectively intervene. The referral was done from June, but, similar to the school, this was one of the cases we were unable to pick up straight away as it was difficult contacting the parents.

They, Mr. and Mrs. Carter, mentioned nothing of this lack of communication with the school, but they did mention that he would always come home with a note in his planner to say he had been crying. They had to go to his school on several occasions as the teachers have raised concerns about how unhappy he was.

Mr. Carter would constantly repeat 'I don't understand why he keeps crying. Men are not allowed to cry. Not the men in my family. Not Black men!'

Suddenly my mind waltzed into memories of my childhood. That day Jah told me he hated me, he was told not to cry. I remember it. I remembered all the tears which were shed in quick secrecy because boys were not allowed to cry. I remembered how angry my brother became because he was never allowed to cry. He was never allowed to talk through his pain.

I couldn't sit back and allow Mr. Carter to pass on his trauma to his son. I responded to him and let him know, respectfully, tactfully, that his son was still a boy and he needed to be allowed to feel as though he could freely cry.

Tears, within the Black home, were taught to be a sign of weakness, but what if these tears were strength? The strength to prevent a boy balling his fists and running them through someone else's body? What if these tears were the definition of being able to not give in to suicidal thoughts? What if these tears were the only way to communicate that there were deeper rooted issues?

Having said this to Mr. Carter, he sank into his seat with eyes steadfast on his feet. His son, Ty, looked up briefly to make eye contact with me. His eyes, though I only saw them for that short moment, told me thanks for understanding him. There was more going on with him, but I wouldn't be able to get it all out of him today. That being said, I scheduled a meeting with them for tomorrow.

It had been a long day not only for myself, but with it being sprung on them that they have a new family coach last minute, it was be best for us to start afresh.

It's that time now. Tomorrow I will be able to let you know more about how this conversation about boys crying ends.

And, on that note. I'm going to bed.

Goodnight Orion.

With purpose, I am signing that my crown is cherished.

Niyah Adenike Thomas.

<u>Date: Tuesday 4th September 2019</u>
<u>Time: 13:45</u>

Affirmations
1 – I no longer walk with negativity hanging from me for I am blessed.
2 – There is no-one out there who owes me their time but me.
3 – Beliefs are constructs which guide us, I believe I am deserving of love. It starts with me.

Dear Orion,

The day is still far from over, but I've made it through my meeting with the Carters. I had no idea it would have been as difficult as it was so I'm thankful that God got me through it. I was fortunate enough to not have anything else in my diary this morning or I would have had to find a way to end the meeting without any hard feelings.

Mr. Carter was adamant that I was wrong with what I said and was certain it would harm Ty if he fell for my belief. Mrs. Carter, once more, sat in silence. Her back slightly turned to her husband, arms crossed across her chest, and legs crossed away from him. She was not happy with the meeting. She was not interested in what her husband had to say.

I allowed him to carry on his tirade. He wasn't in any way being abusive, so I let him feel as though he was in charge of the meeting. It was in his best interest to keep it that way. I trusted that once speaking and allowing it to flow from his chest, he would no longer be burdened by it, allowing me to continue with the session.

'You don't have any right telling me that my son is still a boy.' was one of his arguments. Had I been watching this play out on TV, or had someone told me about it,

I would have been laughing uncontrollably. He failed to see his son as the young boy that he was, one who had barely crossed over into his teenage years, voice not yet broken. Mr. Carter was delusional to say the least.

I wouldn't be the least bit surprised if he hated me after today's meeting. He took 20 minutes of the time telling me how wrong I am, but that he was still willing to work with me. If I'm not mistaken, I do think he said that in time I will understand what he means.

I rounded up his many arguments with 'Mr. Carter, I understand your concerns, and we will in time be able to go through them.' His wife gave me the look. The look which said girl now you know you don't mean that. I smiled softly, letting her know that I knew what I was doing and she needn't worry, but also letting him feel as though he had managed to break me.

Looking over at Ty, I decided to send him outside so I would be able to talk to his parents. Before he left, I quickly explained to everyone that I'd be doing this session a little different, and other sessions may be similar. I worked through the spiel of confidentiality, that if Ty said anything to me that he was unable to share when we all got back together but I felt it raised any concerns, so long as they weren't the ones putting him at risk I would mention it to them.

He left with his hood over his hung head, no eye contact and slumped shoulders. His body language screamed exhaustion.

Ty was barely out the door before Mrs. Carter jumped in with, 'this man, he has killed our son's spirit and I no longer know who my boy is'. Her body rolled, back turned to him a lot more than before. She was at her end. She had hit breaking point.

'In here we will not be blaming anyone for anything.' A well used phrase in my field of work. 'We are here to understand what it is that has been happening and how to work towards a healthy relationship between you all.' Neither party wanted to hear that. I don't blame them. Had someone told me that I'm not allowed to blame the person who was at fault, I'd have been mad too.

It was a difficult session to get through. Mr. Carter had unresolved childhood issues, lessons he learnt which needed to be unlearnt whilst Mrs. Carter was tired of being the target for him to unleash his frustrations. Ty, when we spoke, was tired of hearing his parents argue and in the last academic year, being in a new environment without his friends around him, it was all too much for him to handle.

My target for the family was to write an affirmation for themselves at the beginning of each day with an additional affirmation for the family at the end of the day. The second target they had was to be done together in order to allow them to think about how good they can be as a team and think about the positive things they all are deserving of.

I gave Ty a journal in which he would write negative and positive things which had happened to him throughout the day. His parents were not allowed to look at this journal until they returned for the following session.

The journal Ty received was set out something like this:

Day 1: List all the negative things that happened. Choose one of the negative points and write about how you responded to it. Once you have done that, write one positive thing that happened today.

Day 2: List all the negative things that happened. Choose two negative points and write about how you responded to it. Once you have done that, write two positive things that happened today.

You get it right? Day 3 he is to list all negative things

and choose three points. At the end, he should write 3 positive things which happened.

This would continue to day 7 when they return to meet with me. I imagine this would be good for him. It will allow him to write everything down which he has on his mind. All the concerns he has and how they have manifested as negative things. It would then allow him to think about how he responded to these negatives, but then counteract it with positive outlooks.

Don't get me wrong, I'm not saying that having a positive outlook in life will always allow us to battle the negative reactions, but it would help. Some days will be easier than others.

I'm going to run off now.

With purpose, I am signing that my crown is cherished.

Niyah Adenike Thomas.

<u>Date: Wednesday 5th September 2019</u>

Affirmations
1 – I am doing my best with everything given to me.
2 – I am in love with who I have become.
3 – I am constantly growing.

Dear Orion,

I am grateful for today. It wasn't a difficult day per se, but it wasn't easy. If I could have ensured that it would have been smooth sailing, I would have. However, we all know I don't have that say in life.

The affirmations I have written are related to today. They are the words I have had to tell myself throughout the day. Work was a drag, and that's where the problem lay. The subject of my cousin Ricardo came up at 9:30am and I had lost myself ever since.

Sandra sent me a message for me to see her in her office, and little did I know, it would have revolved around him. I would have preferred if she had told me that my hair was too nappy for work and I needed to look professional for the clients. I would have preferred her having an issue with the way I chose to run yesterday's session.

I didn't expect to see the police sitting in her office with her. It's not how I wanted things to be.

I would have even preferred if the police were there to discuss the Carters and tell me that there were issues there last night. Ask me if I had any information to help. Instead, they needed my help to put my cousin away.

One of the officers mentioned that it had been brought to their attention that Ricardo was a good for nothing, shouldn't have been born, so-called man. That's how it translated in my head at least. What they really said was that he was being investigated for the abuse of

Avery, my little cousin, his niece, and were aware that he had a session with us, with me.

The initial shock did leave me frozen for a short while. The police were there to talk about Ricardo molesting Avery. How did they know? Why show up here and not my home? Why not my parents, or his brother's?

I looked over at Sandra hoping she would give me more and she did. She wasn't as cold hearted as she would have been on a normal day. Today wasn't normal. It was far from it.

'He was seeing a therapist who he told that you knew about him.'

Makes sense. It does, right? When he came in he wasn't happy that I suggested seeing someone else. I was foolish to believe that would have helped him. He wanted to drag me under with him.

I should have turned him in the instant he came in and mentioned that he was seeing someone whose kids he couldn't trust himself around. Instead, I wanted to protect him. Protect him. I wanted to protect the man who molested me as a child. I wanted to protect the man who molested his niece. Now it's come to bite me in the rear end. It's come to bite me in the ass.

I wouldn't be able to talk about this with Sharon present though. I wouldn't be able to tell the truth with my manager in the room. If I started to talk about Avery I would need to tell them about me. I'd have to be honest. There was no way I'd be able to withhold that information.

Sandra recognised my discomfort and suggested that she would head out and cover my caseload for the day. My body exhaled, relieved. Once she had left and closed the door behind her, I was free to talk.

'I'm sorry', I began.

'What for?' Officer 2 asked.

'I'm sorry for my silence' I continued, 'It's just a shock that you are here to ask about my cousin.'

'That's okay.' Officer 2 responded. The soft lines around his eyes spoke care. He wasn't in the job for the sake of it. He was in it because he cared. He looked as though he was ready to take my hands in his and tell me that everything would work out well.

How could I tell them without guilt wrapping itself around my vocal cords that my cousin has taken his time with his niece? Why is it that I know about this and have never reported it? Would I then lose my job for not saying anything? If he had not done anything to these children, was he wrong? The fact I knew about how he felt, was that a bad thing? Should I have sounded the alarm?

I wondered if being honest at that moment would get me shunned once again by the family. I guess at this point I was more able to deal with the family shutting me out than when I was younger. It was too late for me to deny knowing anything but it was also important that I did what needed to be done to prevent it from ever happening again.

Call me the family snitch, but I wouldn't want for him to do to others what he has done to me or Avery. I had the opportunity to make a change. An opportunity to put a pause on his misdemeanours. Justice needed to be served. It was time.

I had some understanding of the law around reporting cases of child abuse, and here I was. I was now putting my job on the line. To be quite honest, I don't know why it was that I felt nervous. I had done my civic duty, contacted the police the day he came in to see me. It was then that I knew he needed to be stopped. It's just the case wasn't taken any further at the time after I had spoken to one of the officers.

I took a deep breath before I began.

'Please accept our apologies. We had not received information about the case from our colleague or we would have been here sooner.'

Deflated with red puffy eyes, I nodded. Accepting their apology, I wondered if the case had fallen on deaf ears because I was Black. Did they not care because my Black cousin was bound to be fondled? Did they decide that it was okay because she wasn't in immediate danger so the case needn't be looked into? Or was it because I mentioned that her parents had since banned him from being around their child?

Whatever it was, I know the weight is now off my chest.

Why I didn't say anything to you, well, I didn't want to remind myself that I would be the family snitch. Telling you then would have meant that I had to come to terms with it all.

And that was how my day went. How about you?

Once more, it's with purpose I am signing that my crown is cherished.

Niyah Adenike Thomas.

A wish upon a constellation,
Granted to a lone star,
One who belongs,
But looked at separately.

Affirmations
1 – I am love.
2 – I am a Queen with a heart like no other.
3 – I am from a line of warriors and I will end generational curses.

Dear Orion,

I received a text today from Charlene to say that she heard that Ricardo had been arrested for child abuse. Never before have I felt nerves shoot through my body, electrocuting me, the way they had done when I received that text.

I was to be relieved, but I knew he'd have known that I spoke. I felt like little Niyah again. The young girl wanting to be accepted by her cousins. By letting the authorities know the truth, the right thing was done, but that little girl in me was still not healed. She was scared, and her fears, shook my body.

The one thing I couldn't stop myself from doing was questioning everything. Did he want to be caught? Did he set himself up? Was this his way to ask for help? Would he be able to get help behind bars?

I do hope that all generational curses which would have followed him will now be healed. I hope he is able to talk things through with a counsellor, you know, come face to face with the demons that have influenced his actions over the years.

Today became the first time I prayed in years. I sent up a prayer for Avery, hoping she would now be able to feel free. It wasn't her who caused her uncle to be arrested, so she wouldn't have that weight to walk with.

That was my burden and I will work towards healing from it, knowing I have now done the right thing.

In the middle of the sitting room is where I knelt down, hands clasped with head to sky. I spoke to God, apologised for having forsaken him for so many years. I needed Him to protect and comfort Avery. I don't know how I'd tell her that for many years I was too a victim of her uncle's warped ideals. This is the reason why God needed to intercede. Without Him, Avery may become victim to her mind's stories about what led to Ricardo being arrested.

Once prayer was done, the weight still loitered. It pressed heavily against my chest. Something within my psyche was different this time around. Historically whenever anything made me as uncomfortable, anxious, and prodded at my depression, I'd want to see Kyron, or drink my sorrows away. This time around though, as the thoughts swirled around in my mind, it was meditation which I went to.

Who would have thought that the family coach Niyah would no longer want to strip down for a man to feel the swells of escapism? I can't say that the weight has completely left me, but there are pieces of me which feel healed.

What has continued to nag at me is that I must be honest with my family. For me to heal I must be honest. Avery must understand that there is someone who understands. Someone who has been through the same. For me to heal, I must aid with her healing that she may have a clearer path than I have.

Family secrets are detrimental. No-one gains anything from keeping them.

On this journey, I pray God guides me so that I may cause no harm to any innocent beings.

Lips sealed are envelopes unopened,
Shunned to collect dust
With secrets, like paper disintegrating.
It's the souls unheard which break,
Little fragments chipped away as time goes by,
No lullaby could soothe the inner child.
All lullabies have dark undertones
Under which the inner child hides,
No longer contemplating murder,
For they have been buried along with the truth,
The reality that we should be better,
But this, like infection left to linger, spreads.
This, like cancer untreated, spreads.

I don't want to be disease ridden
With sores coming to life,
Being manifested through actions,
Mistakes which can never be rectified.
My child is off in heaven wondering why;
Why mommy never stood the chance to escape,
Why mommy never knew her true place,
Why mommy never had strength to allow them
to grow,
Why mommy never healed.

I wish to be wishes,
Like dandelions blown.
I wish to make amends,
The ills I held onto for sake of being forsaken.
I wish to expose.
I wish to be the truthful liar,

Changing the exposure of the photo we have
taken.
Beneath the darkness,
What should come to light?
I wish to be freed.

That's going to be it from me for now Orion. See you tomorrow, maybe a different time, but definitely the same place.

With purpose, I am signing that my crown is cherished.

Niyah Adenike Thomas

<u>Date:</u> Friday 7th September 2019
<u>Time:</u> 7:07pm

Affirmations
1 – I will overcome their traumas.
2 – I will learn how to heal.
3 – I am deserving of all blessings made for me.

Dear Orion,

Would you look at that, only 7 minutes later than yesterday. I commend myself, though I wasn't particularly trying to be back at 7. It just so happened that I have managed to finish all I needed to do today before sitting down with you. Also, a guest, Marcel, is expected to pop by later on and I want to talk to you first.

I've decided that I will meet with Avery and her parents tomorrow. There is no way I can leave this any longer. I don't think I'll be able to forgive myself if I continued life without this conversation. She needs to know that someone understands what she has been through, and her parents do need to know how this could affect her mentally.

I wish my parents understood, or had an idea of how my distress would have impacted me over the years. I wish they had known then that it was the trauma which led to my hospitalisation. I am happy though that life has taught me the lessons I needed to learn to get to where I am today.

To hold on to something which does not serve you leads to more harm than it does good. When a child is taught to sweep under the carpet any harm which has been done to them, they pick up bad habits to cope with the resentment they feel towards themselves. They learn to question everything and develop a taste of bitterness towards others. They learn how to keep away from trusting others who try to come into their lives to love and support them.

The biggest lesson they learn is that they are only deserving of punishment and nothing good is to happen to them.

Children who have been taught to disguise abuse, becoming adults with unhealed pains. An unhealed adult has toxic traits, but believes that they are toxic as a person. They do not understand that they are more than their situations. At times, they aren't aware of their characteristics which were birthed out of the unhealthy lessons they were subjected to learn. They then become the parents who teach their children how to operate out of fear.

If I can have an impact on a little girl to aid in her healing, I want that little girl to be Avery.

Generational curses come from harboured mishaps which manifest themselves in poor behaviour. I want the pattern to end with me. I do not want my children, any other children, to be affected. I need to mend the past. I will be the droplet of water which makes a difference.

Confession #3:

I am being pulled into his essence.
When you look at royalty
Do they make your heart skip beats?
Can you survive when you look at them?

My heart stays still.
I yearn to skip survival mode,
For I still love.

He gives me the energy I need,
Conceals my gratitude for someone like him.
For him, my heart leaps,
Though my body's bound by awe.

I call him King,
To him I am Queen,
Our royalty supersedes oppression

<u>Monday 16th September 2019</u>
<u>Time 21:21</u>

Affirmations
1 – Love is, and always will be, my hope.
2 – I will respect my peace.
3 – How I feel towards something, positive or negative,
will not disrupt my flow.
4 – I will no longer be hard on myself if I somehow stop.
5 – The mornings are my home of abundance, I will rise
and accept them with an open heart.
6 – No longer will I question the signs and confirmations
which meet me daily.
7 – I will let him love me in a way which is right.

Dear Orion,

I'm now ready for a true romantic relationship. I've met the man with qualities that are endearing and honest. He doesn't give me butterflies in my gut. Instead, my nerve endings get excited for the enlightening conversation he and I are bound to have. Souls meeting rather than physical bodies. Qualities of him have always presented themselves in previous guys I have dated, but it's different to see them all in him.

When it came to other guys, I would tell someone about them. But, with him, these past nine days have been exceptional, yet I've told no-one about him. He has been my secret as I've enjoyed the time I've managed to spend with him.

The air about him has been one which I've found to be indescribable, and I have been unquestionably comfortable around him. He makes me feel safe, and I can say I couldn't have asked for better.

Conversations are important to us both. We get to

delve into the topics hidden by our shadows, unpick them. We've vowed to be open with each other. The old me wouldn't have been sure of how to be open with him. I wouldn't have known how much of my past to share with him or how to begin explaining my emotions to him. There has been a shift in me and I am enjoying it. The more we spoke, the more I'd open up to him without second guessing myself. It's an uphill battle though and I think he is aware of this nevertheless, he's been exceptionally patient with me.

How much more could a woman ask for? I've for so long had a hole burning within, unknowingly. Now, I've had someone who allows me to see how much I have healed and understand what it was that I was missing.

This King is someone my parents would love to meet. He is a man whose love is second to none. I have been able to recognise it as honest and genuine because I've seen enough of what love is not. The examples that have previously been presented to me, they taught me what to not accept.

I know it's still early, but I can just tell.

By the way, it's not Marcel. I know he could possibly pass as a potential for me, I've been told, but no, it's not him. I tell you this because, this is also a guy, a man, I have known for some years now.

Our paths have crossed on several occasions. We've spoken, but it wasn't until that Saturday after I had spoken with Avery and her parents that we bumped into each other again.

I left my cousin's house and just before I got in the car I saw him leaving a house on the other side of the road. He waved at me, I was courteous enough to wave back. Opening my door, he called my name and stopped me. I could have told him I had to go, I really did want to get home and decompress after the conversation that had taken place, but I couldn't find the words to tell him I needed to go.

'You know Josh?' he asked, approaching me.

My head tilted, eyebrows furrowed. 'Yeah' I replied, 'How do you know him?'

'I went to school with his brother, Ricardo.'

A lump formed in my throat at the mention of his name. I nodded as to not show, I hoped, that the name Ricardo was a sore topic.

'How do you know them?' he proceeded to ask.

'My cousins.' I bowed my head, this was not a conversation I wanted to engage in. 'Look, Orion, it's nice to see you, but I've –'

He interrupted me. He raised his hand, stopped me mid-sentence. I'm not sure if I should have felt offended.

'I heard what happened to Ricardo. Tough pill to swallow, but I'm not surprised.' By this time he had taken my hand in his. I don't know what was happening, but I was not objecting to it.

No, he didn't come back here with me, and we didn't kiss. We still haven't kissed just yet. Anyway, back to what I was saying, he was holding my hand, staring into the depths of my eyes.

'I don't know how you feel about him being taken in, but it needed to happen.'

That was the key sentence. That was the confirmation I needed. All this time I found it difficult. I still had pieces of me feeling sick for having confessed about him. Hence to hear these words come from someone who knew nothing of my situation with my cousin, it gave me hope and I gave him my number.

Orion, I've waited for the day when I'd meet a guy who makes me feel in the present moment, instead of leaving me to process how I felt. I know if I am angry due to something he says, I feel it in the moment. I process it in the moment. I then determine if I need to deal with it in that moment or let it subside on its own. We have had some small disagreements and I was able to feel and process there and then. I have also been able to discuss it with him and we figure it out together.

I know we won't always agree on things and even when we do disagree, there won't always be a resolution with which we are both happy with.

I do feel as though I've told him all my secrets come to think about it. His name is the one I had chosen to give to you back in July, Thursday 25th to be precise. That could be the reason for my feeling so comfortable with him also, whatever it is, I can honestly say, I love it.

When not blessed by his presence, I find myself thinking about a future with him, including the wedding we would have. It's nothing we've yet spoken about, but he does make me feel and to be able to do so, is key. I've spent enough time being numb. Now, I'm ready to allow my healing to transform my life ahead of me.

A celebrity had compared marriage to coffee and I think I like it. I have taken some time to acquire the taste of coffee and I believe marriage will be the same.

Well, this I've not done in some days now, but, it's with purpose I sign that my crown is cherished.

I'll talk to you again soon.

Niyah Adenike Thomas.

Love in Black

No love exists without understanding,
Standing before reflections in mirrors,
Seeing in ourselves what we wouldn't tolerate in others.

No love finds the world until the world opens,
Arms extended to be cloaked fully,
To take on the joy.

Friday 18th September 2019

In me is a world hidden from the galaxy.
I hold closely what has damaged my internal structures,
But I am working to make repairs.
I know what needs to be extracted,
I guess I'll start there first.

Saturday 19th September 2019

If I were to do this again
I'd smile more,
I'd speak more,
I'd fight more.

I'd fight for my right to speak,
I'd speak better to myself,
I'd have no cloud defeat me.

I'd teach myself my worth.
Only I know my honest worth,
It's tied to my soul,
No-one else knows my soul the way I do.

If I were to do this again,
His room would not be the playground I ventured into,
It would not be the time warped land I got trapped in,
It would not be the lesson I was forced to learn,
It would not be the fight I needed to have.

If I were to do this again,
He would not be my pain,
Or anyone else's.

Jul.2020

Jul. 2020

Dear Orion,

Want to know why this is the name I chose to give to you? I love to look out into the night sky and get lost, on one too many occasions, in The Orion's Belt. By naming you Orion, I've given myself the opportunity to lose my thoughts on paper like I did in the stars, and that I did.

You have been all ears when I felt my words would bounce back had I spoken to anyone else. To have given you so much of me, I've been open to receiving what I felt was missing. There is a depth of love which I had always found difficult to understand and I've still not put my finger on it. However, with the self-confidence and self-love I have regained by speaking to you, I know that greater depth is beyond my understanding and I do not wish to lose out on the love I have now gained by chasing it. It's a process I wish to allow to happen.

I'm like that friend who dumps her friends at the beginning of a new relationship and then runs back to them when things are going wrong. I am so sorry about that. But, I must say, nothing is going wrong. He proposed to me in January of this year and I couldn't say no. The warmth this man brought into my life was the light within that I smothered. He has managed to reignite a lot within me.

There was a sense of familiarity with him, not one I can recall from my past, but one I may have had in a past life. I still think it's because I called you Orion, not knowing I was writing to my future husband.

He shredded my fears about love and with every passing day, I smile at the way he makes me feel. We are equals.

Don't get me wrong, in the beginning we fought. We fought hard. We fought for what we individually thought was right. It only lasted for a week but was long enough to force us into submission.

We made ourselves tired. We drained each other. As a result, we agreed on one thing, we needed some time apart.

It wasn't a break, it was more of us navigating on our own to allow breathing space. I didn't know how to be in a relationship with anyone and he had been single for some time. Mutually, we decided that we needed to pause and figure out who we were as individuals to help decide who we needed to be together. I wanted this to work. He wanted us to work. We needed it. We had spent so much time with each other it led to us losing ourselves completely.

We took a week as our leave of absence. After that week was done, we sat together, as friends, and spoke. We spoke to each other about each other. We spoke into each other's being. We spoke with life. We learnt. We discussed ways to move forward together without the shouting and the screaming. We discussed a future where we would not write the wrongs of our ancestors who were misled and place that into our lives. To learn from their mistakes was key, but we wouldn't repeat them.

Love is our epicentre.

What I love about him is what I love about myself. I love how patient he is with me. He doesn't rush into trying to understand how I am feeling. Instead, he waits. He waits for me to open up to him. He gives me the room to lay my heart on the table and he treats it with care.

I am a lover of his ability to teach. I learn something new from him each day. One of the most poignant lessons he has shared with me is that I should not try to accomplish everything in one breath. Instead, take a moment to enjoy the process taken to achieving each goal.

This was one of those lessons learnt previously, but

the lesson didn't stick with me very much until then.

It took me a moment when he said it, for me to understand why it resonated so well with me. Then I remembered my journal entry on Saturday 3rd August last year. His instructions come with a lasting bliss. I have to admit, some of his train of thoughts I can't bring myself to agree with. Nevertheless, I am all the same grateful for them. They challenge me to find out what it is within me for which I should stand true.

I adore the way he loves his mother. She is his Queen and he treats her with the highest regard. I have witnessed his father doing the same and it's shown me everything that I need to know. He does the same for me because it is something he has taken from his childhood. We are all but beings needing to be elevated by our equals. I cannot help but to return to him the royal treatment he gives to me.

I could not have asked for a more present King to explore love with.

Orion, I thank you for being the counsellor I have always been needing. I wouldn't write off paying for sessions with a counsellor, but it was much cheaper and easier for me to buy a notebook and write to you each day. My mind would not have allowed me to go through counselling. Being honest with someone who is paid to help me is something I will need to talk myself into. Maybe something else for me to explore on another occasion.

> Maybe love isn't so bad,
> Maybe childhood was a good teacher,
> Maybe Jah wasn't wrong after all,
> Maybe we all had to grow first,
> Maybe my relationships weren't all bad,
> Maybe I needed to be kinder to myself,
> Maybe I wasn't mature enough to understand,
> Maybe my grandparents were not wrong,

Love in Black

Maybe they were not one hundred percent right.
Maybe all names have their own power,
Maybe we are inspired when we understand,
Maybe the meanings of our names play bigger parts,
Maybe life is a fantasy misunderstood,
Maybe my name helped me to grow.

I waited for a love to find its way to me
Not knowing I was the love he waited for,
Bound by the unseen heavily repairing our fragments,
We were healed as best as we could on our own.

Maybe we needed each other,
Maybe the final step will be our last day together.

Well Orion, this is the last time I'll be saying this.

With purpose, I'm signing that my crown is cherished.

Niyah Adenike Thomas.

Thank you

I just want to say thank you for not only buying a copy, but also reading it! I just want to ask you if you could do some things for me please, any or all of the following:

1) Leave a review on Amazon.
2) Leave a testimonial on the website www.loveinblack.co.uk/the-book (scroll to the bottom)
3) Share with family and friends on Instagram (Tag me! @careen _latoya or @4dhouseltd or @loveinblackpodcast) 4) Share with family and friends on Facebook
5) Tell the world on TikTok
6) Tell everyone on Twitter

I really appreciate your love and support.

Thank you again.

www.loveinblack.co.uk
www.4dhouseltd.com
www.careenlatoya.com
IG: @loveinblackpodcast
IG: @4dhouseltd
IG: @careen_latoya

4D HOUSE

Exhale Publishing

Lightning Source UK Ltd.
Milton Keynes UK
UKHW040947070921
390143UK00001B/4